LOVE IN LANCASTER COUNTY

WHEN SUNLIGHT FALLS

· Johnnie Alexander ·

Annie's®

Books in the Love in Lancaster County series

A Promise Kept
Fields of Promise
When Sunlight Falls

. . . and more to come!

Library of Congress-in-Publication Data
When Sunlight Falls / by Johnnie Alexander
p. cm.
I. Title
                          2021944308

AnniesFiction.com
(800) 282-6643
Love in Lancaster County™
Series Creator: Shari Lohner

10 11 12 13 14 | Printed in China | 9 8 7 6 5 4 3 2 1

CHAPTER ONE

Snowflakes lazily floated onto muddy slush piles, covering the gray mess with a layer of white. This was a common sight, and part of a familiar weather cycle, in the small town of Birdsong Falls, in Lancaster County, Pennsylvania. As soon as the first snowfall of winter arrived, the heavy tires of cars and buggies soiled the smooth blanket, and slow-moving plows pushed its melting remnants to the curbs. Then, even before the old snow had completely melted away, more snow fell and restored the town's picturesque beauty. At least for a little while.

As she drew close to the Bouquet Bliss Florist Shop, Talitha Byler halted her horse in the middle of Birch Street and waited for an opening in the traffic so that she could turn left into the alley beside the shop. A young *Englisch* girl, probably no more than four or five years old, stood on the sidewalk to the right of the buggy. When the child, wearing bright red mittens, waved at her, Tally returned the wave with a warm smile.

When the traffic cleared, Tally guided Sprout to make the turn. A fresh blanket of snow covered the alley's dirt path, and she wished she didn't have to spoil it with her horse's hooves and buggy wheels. But she had no choice: the poinsettia plants she'd grown for Christmas needed to be delivered.

Sprout stopped beside the shop's side door without any prompting. He'd made this stop often enough to know Tally's routine. She climbed down from the seat, then grabbed the side of the buggy as her feet slid on a patch of ice. She'd need to be careful if she didn't want to land on her backside. What would her grandparents have to say about that?

With halting steps, she walked to the other side of the buggy and pulled one of the poinsettia boxes from its floor. Thick red leaves towered over the box packed with nine pots. Tally had selected the best plants in her greenhouse for Amanda Collins, the Englisch woman who owned the florist shop. Tally owed her interest in growing and selling flowers to Mrs. Collins's encouragement and support.

As Tally started for the shop's side door, a loud cry caught her attention. She gingerly stepped to the corner of the alley and looked across Birch Street. The little girl who'd waved to her was struggling to get away from a woman who was clutching her hand.

Tally headed toward the street as she tried to make sense of the situation. Suddenly, tires squealed, and a sedan braked hard in the far lane. Tally noticed the cause immediately: a bedraggled puppy, now cowering in front of the car. While Tally watched, the child slipped her hand from her mitten, escaping the woman's grip, and ran toward the street. As the woman snatched up the child, the puppy scurried toward Tally's side of the road, just as another vehicle was approaching.

Without thinking, Tally dropped the box of poinsettias and raced into the street. She grabbed the puppy, which had reached the lane closest to her, just as there came another screech of tires. The oncoming car fishtailed, its rear bumper swinging toward her as she jumped back to the sidewalk.

Time seemed to slow as she struggled to catch her breath. The box lay on its side on the ground. Poinsettia leaves were strewn among the clay debris on the snowy sidewalk. Tally cuddled the damp puppy close and looked across the street. The woman held the girl in her arms. Her expression was one of great relief.

Everyone was safe.

"Is he yours?" Tally shouted to the woman.

"What's wrong with you?" The car that had barely missed Tally was now stopped by the sidewalk in front of the florist shop. The driver, peering through the passenger side window, sounded distraught. "You could have been killed."

"I'm sorry," Tally stammered. "The puppy . . ."

The man let out a long breath, which seemed to dispel his anger. "No harm done as long as you're both okay."

The woman with the girl and the occupants of the first car that had stopped came across the street toward Tally. The sidewalk was crowded with bystanders who'd spilled out from the nearby stores. Clutching the puppy close to her cloth coat, Tally took a step back and then another. One more step and then her boot hit an icy patch beneath the thin layer of snow.

Immediately, Tally went down on her backside among the red poinsettia leaves. She closed her eyes, wishing a hole would open in the sidewalk for her to disappear into forever. The puppy wiggled and licked her chin, his tongue scratchy and warm. A murmur of voices surrounded her. She opened her eyes to find what felt like a gazillion smartphones pointed in her direction.

Strangers taking her photo? This couldn't be happening. She closed her eyes again and prayed that her grandparents would never find out about her misadventure. Embarrassment already felt like a weight on her chest. Their disapproval would only make things worse. "Never draw attention to yourself" was practically a family motto. In her grandparents' eyes, there was no difference between purposeful attention and accidental attention. It didn't matter how or why Tally had drawn a crowd like this. The blame would fall on her shoulders.

The bell over the florist shop door tinkled as Mrs. Collins scurried through it. Her eyes filled with concern as she knelt beside Tally. "Are you okay? Anything bleeding? Broken?"

"I don't think so." Tally groaned as she pushed herself into a sitting position. Her stomach dropped at the sight of the poinsettia leaves and smashed pots. She'd spent so much time tending and nurturing the plants—and they'd ended up like this!

Oblivious to Tally's misery, the puppy circled in her lap, lay down on her now-muddy skirt, and closed his eyes. She scooped him up and nestled him against her shoulder. "No sleeping for you, little man. You're the one who caused this mess." Once again, he licked her chin.

Mrs. Collins's worried expression eased into a smile as she straightened the white *Kapp* on Tally's head. "Let's get you both inside," she said. "Do you think you can stand?"

Before Tally could answer, Nicole Collins emerged from the florist shop, waving her cell phone. "Should I call 911?"

"I don't think that will be necessary," Mrs. Collins said to her daughter. Nicole was nineteen years old, the same as Tally. They'd been friends since the day they met at a county flower show as preteens. "Let's get Tally to her feet."

Nicole took the puppy from Tally as Mrs. Collins and the child's mother helped her stand.

"What's your puppy's name?" Tally asked the little girl.

"He's not ours," the mother said. "I don't know where he came from."

"Wow, Tally. It looks like you got an early Christmas present," Nicole teased.

"I wish." Tally scratched the puppy behind his silky ears and imagined the horrified reaction she'd get if she took him home.

"That was a brave thing you did," the mother said. "Are you sure you aren't hurt? Is there anything I can do?"

Tally shifted her gaze from the puppy to the woman. "Do you want to take him?"

"I wish I could, but we're a cat family." She glanced at her watch. "Sorry, we need to go. I'm glad you're okay."

As Mrs. Collins ushered the girls into the store, Tally glanced over her shoulder at the wreckage left behind on the sidewalk. "I'm sorry about the poinsettias," she said. "I didn't mean to drop them. But the puppy . . ."

"Don't worry your head about that," Mrs. Collins said. "Poinsettias can be replaced. But not you, and not runaway puppies."

"I have four more boxes in the buggy."

"We'll get them later. Right now, I think we can all use a hot cup of chamomile tea." Mrs. Collins escorted Tally past the shop's bright and cheery Christmas displays to the break room in the back of the store. "Let me help you with that coat, then you take a seat. The tea will be ready in a few minutes."

Tally lowered herself to the upholstered couch. Her backside and shoulders ached, her clothing was muddied, and her dignity had taken a blow. Thankfully, she didn't seem to have any serious injuries. Nicole handed the puppy, now wrapped in a towel she'd grabbed from the nearby bathroom, to Tally.

"You stay right there," Nicole said in her characteristic take-charge tone. "I'll go see what I can salvage from the Great Poinsettia Splat and Splash. I promise I won't be long. Then you can tell me what exactly happened out there, and we can talk about this cute little fella." She patted the puppy, then hurried off.

Now that she was away from the sidewalk crowd, Tally let out a deep sigh. She still felt horrid about the loss of the poinsettia plants, but she couldn't resist basking in Mrs. Collins's tender care. Nicole was lucky to have such an amazing mother. A pang of jealousy zapped through Tally's heart as it so often did when she was in Amanda Collins's presence. During all the years she and Nicole had been friends, Tally had fought against the poisonous emotion that left her longing for them to trade places. But in the past couple of years, her relationship with Mrs. Collins had changed. She was no longer only Nicole's fabulous mom. She had become Tally's mentor and friend too. That realization had done much to ease Tally's twinges of envy.

In this moment, however, as embarrassment and humiliation swirled within her, Tally's heart ached with the loss of what she'd never had. A *Mamm* to kiss her boo-boos, both real and imaginary, or to hold her tight after a nightmare's scream. A Mamm who would listen to her dreams for the future and hold them close within her own heart.

Tally loved her grandmother, but *Grossmammi* didn't have the imagination or patience for Tally's dreams. She'd given permission for Tally to establish her own plant nursery, but she didn't like the fact that it meant Mrs. Collins held influence over Tally. But *Grossdaddi* had taken Tally's side and not allowed Grossmammi to forbid the relationship.

Tally wasn't sure why this was the case. Perhaps he recognized how much Tally learned from Mrs. Collins and saw how that knowledge improved the quality of her plants. Grossdaddi was a cabinetmaker and a craftsman, and he valued quality in workmanship. Though pride was verboten in the Amish community, Grossdaddi strongly believed that *Gött* expected His followers to do their best work as a way to honor Him.

Mrs. Collins emerged from the shop's kitchenette with two cups of steaming tea. She placed one on the table beside Tally and then sat in a nearby chair, cradling the other. "I was replacing one of the plants in the window display when I heard the squeal of brakes. Oh, Tally. You gave me such a fright when you ran into that street. You could have been seriously injured."

The kindness of her tone warmed Tally's heart as much as the hot tea warmed her insides. "It all happened so fast I didn't stop to think. I had to save him." The puppy, still snug inside the towel, had fallen asleep, the tip of his tongue barely sticking out of his mouth. Beneath Tally's hand, his chest rose and fell with each breath.

"You have a good heart. But sometimes you need to use your head." Mrs. Collins tapped her temple.

If the gentle admonition had come from anyone else, probably even from Grossmammi, Tally would have resented it. But she knew that Mrs. Collins was only saying what she would have said to Nicole if she'd been the one to run into the street. Tally sipped her hot tea carefully and relished the feeling of having been invited into the Collins family sphere.

"Are you sure you're not hurt?" Mrs. Collins asked.

"I'm a little sore where I landed."

"I'm not surprised. I have no idea how you managed to hold on to that puppy while you were going down."

Tally's cheeks warmed. What a spectacle she must have been. No wonder so many people had come out of the nearby stores with their phones.

"If it's any consolation, you fell very gracefully." The corners of Mrs. Collins's mouth turned up in a teasing smile. It was so like this wonderful woman to say the right thing even when it wasn't the unvarnished truth.

Tally tried to recall the split second between the moment she started to slide and the second she landed on the sidewalk. She remembered clutching the puppy close to her chest with one arm while the other spun out of control like the spoke of a runaway wheel. The image made her laugh. "We both know better than that."

"It's my story, and I'm sticking to it." Mrs. Collins pointed at the puppy. "Does he have a collar?"

Tally pulled back the towel and ran her finger around the puppy's neck. "No. But he needs a bath. And he seems thin." For the first time, she took a good look at the sleeping dog. His coat was mostly gray with black splotches, and his chest, stomach, and toes were white. Tan markings around his eyes and muzzle matched the tan fur on his legs. Though his fur was dirty, it was also cottony soft.

"What are you going to do with him?" Mrs. Collins asked.

"Me?" The question surprised Tally. She'd been too busy imagining herself as a part of the Collins family to consider anything else. "I suppose he belongs to someone."

"Not anyone who was out on the street. They would have come into the shop to claim him."

"Maybe he's lost."

Mrs. Collins's warm smile returned. "He looks adorably comfortable in your lap. If he's a stray, you could keep him."

"I'm not sure my grandparents would approve." Tally swallowed a sigh, then gave Mrs. Collins a pleading look. It was a look that had worked for her and Nicole before when they wanted Nicole's mother to say yes to a request. "Why don't you take him? Then I could still see him when I come visit."

Mrs. Collins waved a finger from side to side. "Those big brown eyes aren't going to work this time," she said with a laugh. "There's a good reason we don't already have a dog. Mr. Collins is allergic to almost all animals. Dogs, cats, horses, goats. He has to take an antihistamine before we go to the zoo."

"I guess I'll have to take the puppy home, then. At least for today." Her grandparents wouldn't be happy, but surely if it was just for one night, they wouldn't mind. Maybe one night could turn into two and then three . . .

The problem was, she'd have to tell them *why* she had the puppy. Though perhaps she wouldn't have to tell the entire story.

They'd certainly never see the photos or videos of her lying on the sidewalk with her dress askew, surrounded by the broken pots and strewn poinsettias.

A twinge of guilt needled her, but she swatted it away. This wouldn't be the first time she hadn't told her grandparents every single detail of her day. And it wouldn't be the last. This way of navigating her circumstances, even if her grandparents weren't aware of it, made life easier for all of them.

Nicole rushed into the room, interrupting her musings. "You'll never guess what happened." She waved her phone and plopped on the couch. "You're famous."

Tally steadied the teacup that wobbled as Nicole bounced beside her. "I'm what?"

"Just look." Nicole held out her phone so Tally could see the screen. "Tally's picture is the top post on the *Birdsong Banner* website," she said to her mother as Tally took the phone from her. "She's a hero for saving this sweet baby."

"Already?" Mrs. Collins exclaimed. "I'll never get used to how fast things show up online."

"It only takes a moment for someone to upload a picture." Nicole scratched the pup's head. He opened his eyes, stretched, then snuggled deeper into the towel and resumed his nap. "And another for the paper to send out a news alert."

"I don't believe it." Tally read the headline: *Amish Girl Saves Dog from Certain Death.*

Nothing melodramatic about that.

She read the article's first sentence.

An unidentified girl believed to be from our local Amish district risked life and limb earlier today to rescue a small dog that ran into oncoming traffic on Birch Street.

Great! Her grandparents wouldn't have ever seen the photos on people's cell phones. But someone who recognized Tally might very well tell them about the article. At least the accompanying photo showed her standing on the sidewalk cradling the puppy, and not sprawled among the poinsettias. She prayed that her grandparents would never learn that part of the story.

"You're famous," Nicole said again. "I bet we can charge more for your poinsettias now. Everyone will want a plant grown by the gal who saved the puppy."

Grossdaddi often told Tally to look for the silver lining in any hard situation. Maybe this was one of those times. The plants were sold on commission, so the more the florist shop charged for the poinsettias, the more money Tally earned.

But that would be the only silver lining she'd see if her grandparents ever learned the story the newspaper hadn't told.

CHAPTER TWO

Inside one of the barn's workrooms, Caleb Schwartz propped a hand-cranked corn sheller up on the box he'd made out of a couple of two-by-sixes. Then he placed the entire contraption on top of a sturdy five-gallon bucket as his six-year-old sister stood beside him, watching him work.

"Now can I do it?" Sadie's big blue eyes peered up at him. He couldn't help but chuckle at the little girl's eagerness. All of Sadie's siblings had already reached their teen years by the time she was born. Caleb had been fourteen, Eliza thirteen, and the two older boys were already thinking about who they wanted to court. Now Jonah and Daniel had families of their own.

"Do you remember which end to put in first?" Caleb asked.

Sadie studied the ear of corn she held in her hands, then pointed to the thinner end. "This one."

"That's right. Go ahead now."

Sadie placed the ear into the sheller's opening. Her small face grimaced as she struggled at first with the hand crank, but Caleb knew not to offer help unless she asked for it. Sadie's first sentence as a baby had been "Me do it," a fact that the family still recalled with great amusement.

Once the crank was turning, the kernels started to plop into the bucket. This continued until the bare cob went flying out the sheller's chute. Sadie clapped her hands and ran around the contraption to pick up the cob and remove the few remaining kernels by hand. While she busied herself with that task, Caleb ran three more ears through the sheller so they'd have enough kernels to pop a test batch.

If the kernels popped to the family's satisfaction, then he'd shell the rest of the ears and store the kernels in gallon jars. If not, he'd try again in a week or so. In the spring, Eliza would make up packets of homegrown popcorn to sell at the local farmers' market for a little extra pocket money.

Sadie held the funnel while Caleb poured the kernels into a small jar, filling it about a third of the way. "I want to carry the popcorn," she said.

"You're the only one I'd let carry it." He tapped her on the nose. "But first, we need to put everything away."

Sadie dusted the funnel with a clean cloth and returned it to the proper drawer while Caleb tended to cleaning and storing the rest of the equipment. After all, "doing what's right today means no regrets tomorrow," as their father was fond of saying. *Daed* used that old proverb to cover more than just moral conduct. To him, doing what's right also meant having a place for everything and putting everything in its place, mending a scratch before it became a tear, and leaving everything—both objects used and places visited—better than one found them.

Once the workroom was tidy again, Caleb checked the jar to make sure Sadie had tightened the lid. Though the walk from the barn to the house wasn't a long one, he fastened Sadie's coat and helped her with her mittens. Before they walked out the door, he lifted her to his shoulders as she clutched the jar of popcorn.

The snow from the previous night covered the landscape. The only marks in it were the footprints he and Sadie left when they walked out to the barn and the wagon tracks Daed had left with his buggy when he and Mamm drove off earlier that morning to visit Mamm's sister.

Caleb's heart did a little flip at the sight of Sprout hitched to a familiar buggy in the drive. *Tally.* If he'd known she was here, he would have put off shelling the popcorn. He hoped she wasn't in a hurry to leave.

He hesitated when he reached the screened-in back porch. "Take the popcorn inside to Eliza," he said to Sadie as he set her on her feet. "I'll be there in a minute."

She readily agreed and ran inside, excited to help pop the corn. Once she was gone, Caleb removed his hat and ran his fingers through his hair. Not out of vanity, he assured himself. He only wanted to show that he wasn't slovenly.

Though Tally already knew that about him. They'd known each other for most of their lives. Back when they were *Kinna*, he'd paid little attention to her, or to any of the other girls in their one-room schoolhouse. Once they were *Youngies*, though . . . Caleb let out a long breath at the memory. Well, since then, he hadn't had eyes for anyone else.

He stamped his feet on the outside mat and opened the screened door to the back porch. Sadie's coat lay on the floor beneath its hook. Mamm would have called Sadie back to hang it up, but Mamm wasn't here, so Caleb hung it for her. He heard the sound of voices coming from the nearby kitchen, too soft for him to make out the words. But the hum of Eliza's murmur followed by Tally's laugh warmed his heart. How blessed he was that his sister and the young woman he hoped to spend his life with were the best of friends.

Caleb prepared himself to greet Tally with a cordial smile and hoped she wouldn't hear the pounding of his heart. He stepped into the kitchen and stopped short, surprised by the scene before him.

Tally and Sadie sat on the floor as a mottled gray puppy with intelligent eyes scampered back and forth between them. The dog's body wiggled with excitement, and Sadie giggled when he nipped at the hem of her dress.

"Where did that come from?" Caleb asked.

"Tally rescued him." Eliza stood by the stove, whisking hot cocoa in a saucepan. "He almost got hit by a car."

Caleb's stomach knotted as horrific scenarios flashed through his mind. But none of those things had happened. The proof was before him. Tally sat cross-legged on the pine floor, all in one piece and with no visible sign of injury. Their eyes met, and she flushed, her cheeks turning an attractive shade of pink before she turned her gaze back to the puppy.

Sadie stopped giggling, her face growing serious. "He's not hurt, is he?"

"Look how he's playing." Tally's voice was reassuring. "He's a bit thin, I think, but other than that, he seems fine."

Caleb moved to join the two on the floor, but Eliza shoved the popcorn jar into his hands when he neared the stove.

"Aren't you going to pop this for us?" Her tone betrayed nothing, but her eyes danced with merriment. "Tally and I have been waiting for you to come in from the barn."

"Of course," he said as if that had been his intention all along. Eliza could have her good-natured fun at his expense, but turnabout was fair play. "Too bad Marcus Fisher didn't stop by. He told me that no one makes cocoa like you do." Marcus Fisher, the youngest son of their district's deacon, had made no secret of his admiration for Eliza.

"He did no such thing." Eliza turned away to hide her flush and whisked the cocoa even harder.

"Careful with that." Caleb leaned close and whispered, "Truce?"

Eliza's expression relaxed as she placed the whisk on a spoon holder and reached for a ladle. "Truce," she answered quietly. While Eliza ladled the frothy cocoa into mugs, Caleb heated oil and three kernels in a saucepan. Once those kernels popped, he knew the oil was hot enough to pop more, and he added more to the pan. Usually Sadie would be standing on a chair beside him, watching the kernels transform into fluffy white popcorn, but today the puppy had her transfixed. Caleb forced himself to hold in his curiosity about Tally's rescue until after the kernels stopped popping.

"Looks like the rest of the corn is ready to be shelled," he announced as he poured the pan's contents into a large bowl. "Almost all of the kernels popped. Now who's ready for the taste test?"

"I want to stay with the puppy," Sadie said from the floor.

"It's time for him to take a nap." Tally stood and reached for Sadie's hand. "And we need to help with the tasting. That part is the most fun, don't you think?"

"Besides," Caleb added, "it's my turn to see this little guy. And to hear about his rescue."

"Eliza has already heard the story." Tally handed the puppy to Caleb, then led Sadie to the table.

"He's wet!" Caleb wiped one hand on his pants while cradling the puppy with the other. He grabbed a nearby towel and wrapped it around the dog.

"We had to give him a bath." Eliza plopped a dollop of marshmallow crème into each of the cocoa-filled mugs. "He was a muddy mess, and you should have seen Tally when she came in." Eliza, who couldn't abide the smallest spot or stain on her apron, grimaced. "But I don't mind hearing the story again. Go ahead, Tally."

"There's not much to tell," Tally said as she took her seat at the table. "He was in the street near the florist shop. A car was coming and—"

"Tally ran into the street!" Eliza shuddered. "I would never have been that brave."

Caleb's heart dropped to his stomach. "You ran into the street? You could have been killed."

"I didn't think about that." Tally's defensive tone was softened with something else. Not regret. Caleb was certain that if the same incident occurred tomorrow, she'd do exactly the same thing. Instead, she seemed almost in awe, as if she couldn't quite believe that what had happened had, in fact, happened. "The puppy's fine. I'm fine. That's all that matters."

Caleb wasn't sure he agreed. "It's *gut* you're fine. Was there no traffic?" *Please, God, let there have been no traffic.*

"There was some." Tally bent her head over her bowl. "This popcorn is delicious. I'm sure Grossdaddi will buy a jar. Maybe two."

"I'll put aside two jars for you," Eliza said. "We can trade popcorn for tulip bulbs if you'd like. I especially like the yellow ones you had last spring."

Caleb held up a hand. "Changing the subject won't work. What do you mean by 'there was some' traffic? One vehicle? Five?"

"Only two cars skidded to a stop," Tally said. "Thankfully, the others managed to stop too. It would have been awful if there had been any accidents."

There was more to this story, Caleb could tell. He was determined to find out what details she was omitting.

"That is *gut.*" He kept his tone matter-of-fact. "I think I'll drive into town later today. Maybe even stop in to see Mrs. Collins. Ask her if anything unusual happened outside her store this morning."

Tally glared at him. "There's no need for that." Two red spots highlighted her cheeks. "It's too embarrassing. I can't tell it again."

"She dropped all her poinsettias," Eliza said. "Then she slipped on the sidewalk and landed on her . . ." She turned to Tally, an apologetic expression in her eyes.

But she didn't need to finish the sentence for Caleb to imagine the slip and the landing. He did his best to suppress the laugh that bubbled in his chest, but it was right there, ready to explode at any second.

"My grandparents will be horrified." Tally covered her eyes with both hands.

"They'll never know," Eliza comforted her.

"I think they will."

Her distraught tone dispelled Caleb's humor in a way that his determination to refrain from laughing had not. The elderly Bylers would be grateful Tally hadn't been injured, of course. But he knew that this blessing wouldn't keep them from blaming her for what they would see as reckless and unbecoming behavior.

The Bylers were good people. Hardworking, honest, and respectable. But also inclined to keep to themselves—at least as much as any Amish family could in their district. Aaron Byler helped at the barn raisings, and Iris Byler joined the other women at the quilting bees. They rarely missed the every-other-week church services.

Yet Caleb had long sensed that they did these things because of community expectations. In between these events, they generally stayed home and tended to their own affairs. Caleb had once overheard his parents talking about the Bylers' peculiar ways.

"It's odd," Caleb remembered Mamm saying. "They seem to want to fit in, but it's almost as if they aren't sure how." Daed had suggested that perhaps the standards had been different in the Amish community where they used to live. That was the moment when Caleb learned that the Bylers hadn't always lived in Lancaster County.

He'd later asked Tally where she and her family had moved from, but she'd been even more surprised than he to learn that their Amish community hadn't always been her home. Her grandparents had never talked about living somewhere else. The past was a verboten topic.

"People took photos." Tally's words brought him back to the moment. Her voice sounded muffled, coming from behind the hands she still held to her face. "The *Birdsong Banner* even put one on their website."

"You didn't tell me that," Eliza said in a shocked tone. "That means everyone in town will know."

"Someone is sure to tell Grossdaddi." Tally lowered her hands. She wore an expression of resignation on her face. "I must tell him first. I've postponed going home long enough."

The puppy squirmed in Caleb's arms, and he relaxed his grip, which had grown tense as Tally talked. The thought of strangers taking photos of her had sparked a flame of anger inside him. Now to learn that one of them was online—that fed the flame. The local editor knew the Amish people considered the publishing of their photographs an invasion of their privacy. Why had he made this exception without Tally's permission?

"Your popcorn is very *gut*," Tally said to Caleb as she reached for a canvas bag that sat beside the table. "Your best ever."

"You say that every year." Somehow he managed to keep his voice steady despite the fire burning in his chest.

"Because it's true." Her charming smile dampened his irritation. She brushed her hand against the pristine white of the apron she was wearing. "*Danki* for the clean clothes," she said to Eliza. "I'll return them soon."

"We couldn't have your Grossmammi seeing you covered in slush and with a hole in your stocking." Eliza's eyes twinkled. Her initial shock had quickly passed, and now she seemed amused by the entire situation. But that was how Eliza saw the world. Her glass was always half-full, and the lenses in her wire-rimmed spectacles were tinted with a "see the best in everything" rosiness.

Caleb almost wished he could act as nonchalant as his sister about the situation, but Tally's story had worsened with each new detail. Did the distasteful newspaper photo depict a disheveled Amish girl? *His* disheveled Amish girl?

Admittedly, she wasn't *his* yet. But he had every reason to believe that she would be. He always drove her home after the Sunday evening sings. When the weather allowed, they sat together on the front porch swing. Otherwise, they visited in the parlor. How could he not feel protective of her?

"I wish I had driven you to town," he said. "Then none of this would have happened."

"Are you certain of that?" Tally tapped the puppy's nose. "No matter what, this little guy would have run into the street and I would have gone after him. Maybe tomorrow I can find his owner."

"May I keep him?" Sadie piped up. "He could stay with me forever and ever."

"He probably belongs to someone else who's missing him very much," Eliza said as she wiped a chocolate smudge from Sadie's chin. She didn't say what Caleb knew to be true. Their parents had no interest in raising another dog. The entire family had been devastated when their fifteen-year-old retriever mix had died a couple of years ago. Mamm had taken the loss especially hard and was adamant that there would be no more dogs on the Schwartz farm.

Sadie made a pouty face, but she didn't fuss. Tally let her give the puppy a final hug, then told them all goodbye.

"I'll walk you out." Caleb hoped his smile looked more sincere than he felt. The unsettled feeling in his stomach didn't seem to want to go away.

"I'd like that," Tally replied, then said goodbye to Eliza.

Sadie followed them to the back porch and held the puppy while they put on their coats. Tally had put the canvas bag containing her muddied clothing on the ground, and Caleb picked it up while she persuaded a reluctant Sadie to relinquish her hold on the dog. Sadie's lower lip stuck out in a pout, and they could still hear her shouted goodbyes after they had closed the door behind them.

"You weren't too badly injured, were you?" Caleb asked as they navigated their way to Tally's buggy. "When you fell, I mean?"

She laughed, a small, self-deprecating sound. "It was mostly my dignity that got hurt."

"Am I right in thinking you haven't told me the whole story?"

"You are right." Her cheeks flushed. "I was carrying a box of poinsettias when I saw the puppy. I dropped them, and the containers broke. Nicole called it the Great Poinsettia Splat and Splash."

"That sounds like something Nicole would come up with." Caleb liked the Collins family. Most of the Englisch who lived in the county treated their Amish neighbors with respect and appreciation for their dedication to a way of life they considered unusual. But the friendships the Collins family shared with a few Amish families went even deeper.

Caleb could see that Tally longed for a mother figure in her life, and Amanda Collins definitely fulfilled that need by encouraging her green thumb and helping her establish a business of her own. She'd supported Tally in other ways, too, through the expression of her calm demeanor and sunny outlook on life. Caleb had always admired Nicole's mother, but in the past few years, he'd found many reasons to feel grateful for her maternal regard for Tally.

"Mrs. Collins said it didn't matter." Tally's voice cut into his thoughts. "Nicole salvaged what she could, and we repotted them before I came here. It's still a loss, though."

"Plants don't matter as much as you do." He'd thank Gött every day for the rest of his life that Tally hadn't been hit by one of those cars.

"Or that puppy." She chuckled. "Sadie wanted to name him Scamp. But I suppose he already has a name. He has to belong to somebody. Doesn't he?"

"We can try to find out," Caleb said. "Was he in the photo too?"

"I'm holding him in it." For a moment, Tally seemed lost in thought. "At first, I was upset they had posted the picture. But Nicole said that if the owner sees the story, then they'll know where to find their pet."

"So now you don't mind?"

"Not as much as I did." She pointed to a bag of dog food in the buggy. "Nicole ran out to buy that while I was repotting the plants. He gobbled it up so quickly I was afraid he was going to be sick."

"Maybe he is a stray, then. Though he seems young to be out on his own."

Her eyes brightened with longing. "Is it wrong of me to hope that he doesn't belong to anyone?"

"You want to keep him?"

"Yes," Tally admitted. She glanced away as a deep sigh escaped her lips. "But we both know my grandparents will never allow it. Or if they did, they'd make him stay in the barn."

Caleb widened his eyes. "You want him to live inside the house?"

"Why not? Lots of dogs do."

"Not very many Amish dogs."

"I suppose not." Tally gave him a teasing grin, an expression he savored, and he felt his pulse quicken. "Maybe more of them should."

How could he dispute anything she said when her expressive brown eyes turned his thoughts to mush? "Maybe so."

At his unexpected agreement, her lips widened in a smile that warmed him from the inside out. He would do just about anything to see that smile every day, and he hoped she knew it.

"I promised Daniel I'd help him at his farm tomorrow," he said, "but I'm free on Thursday. If no one contacts you before then, we could go to town together. We'll find who owns this puppy."

"I like that plan. Danki."

"Anytime." He gripped her elbow to help her into the buggy. "Be safe driving home. Promise me. No more spills."

"That would be a piecrust promise," she said in a singsong voice followed by a cute smile.

"Easily made and easily broken," they both said at the same time.

Tally picked up Sprout's reins and then leaned toward Caleb. She gave him a look of mock seriousness. "But I will try."

He stood in the same spot until she'd driven fully out of his sight. How he longed to tell Tally plainly what he thought and what he had planned. His Christmas surprise for her was almost ready. As soon as he finished it, he would ask her the question that burned inside of him.

As far as he was concerned, that day couldn't come quickly enough.

CHAPTER THREE

By the time Tally arrived back home at the Byler farm, she no longer needed to guide Sprout. The gelding gingerly picked his way between the melting slush piled on either side of the drive as he made his way to the horse barn. The knot in Tally's stomach tightened with each rotation of the wagon wheels. She briefly considered hiding the puppy in the barn but dismissed the notion. Such a move wouldn't gain her anything in the long run. Her grandparents would find out what happened soon enough. The *Banner*'s twice-a-week print editions came out on Wednesdays and Sundays. If the paper ran the story, they could be reading it at breakfast tomorrow morning.

Inside the barn, Sprout waited patiently as Tally placed a horse blanket in a wooden box with sides too tall for the puppy to climb over. "Inside you go, you little scamp," she said, placing the little guy in the box. She liked Sadie's choice of a name. Surely it wouldn't hurt to call him that until she found his owner. He squirmed and cried, but she resisted the urge to pick him up again. "Sprout needs my attention now. And you need to learn to settle yourself."

She placed a handful of dog kibble on a clean rag and set it in the box. Scamp sniffed at the food, gave a pitiful yelp, and then lay down with his nose on the corner of the cloth. Tally stifled a chuckle. She hoped he would go to sleep. And that her grandfather wouldn't come out to join her in the barn.

Once Sprout was unharnessed from the buggy, Tally led the gelding to his stall. She added a cupful of feed to the bucket hooked on the wall, then brushed Sprout while he ate his dinner. The puppy whimpered a few times, but Tally did her best to ignore him.

All of her friends in the district came from large families. Not only did Eliza have Sadie and her brothers, but she also had multiple cousins who lived nearby. Tally had no one. No siblings. No cousins. No family at all besides Grossdaddi and Grossmammi.

The questions she rarely allowed herself to ask tugged at her heart.

Where are my parents? What happened to them? Why won't anyone tell me?

These questions seemed to assail her every year in the days leading up to Christmas, perhaps because that's when she most keenly felt that she was missing out on something good and joyful and precious. Other families had huge gatherings and feasts to celebrate the holidays. But her grandparents refused invitations to attend those happy events and never invited anyone to join them in their own home.

In recent years, however, Tally had been allowed to spend part of Christmas Day with Eliza and her family. Tally cherished those times, especially since it meant she also got to spend time with Caleb, who burrowed his way deeper into her heart with each moment they were together.

But despite all the joy his family had given her, it also saddened her to think that all her cheerful holiday memories had come about because other people pitied her circumstances.

A couple of years before, when she and Nicole were discussing Christmas Day plans, Tally had expressed gratitude for the way the Schwartz family included her. Immediately sensing the hurt behind that gratitude, Nicole had hatched a plan to find out the names of Tally's parents and to discover where the Bylers had lived before moving to their Amish community.

Nicole had conducted internet searches, scoured through census records, and asked innocent-sounding questions to long-time residents of Birdsong Falls. But despite her efforts, she'd discovered nothing, and as time passed without any promising leads, her interest in solving the mystery had waned and then dried up completely.

Tally didn't blame Nicole for giving up. Even if her friend had learned anything, what good would it have done? As far as her grandparents were concerned, Tally's parents were a closed book—one they never intended to take from its shelf. Tally doubted she'd ever be able to pry that book open—not even enough to get the tiniest glimpse of its pages. It would take a miracle to make such a thing happen.

Out here in the Byler barn, though, Tally had a different miracle in mind. Somehow she had to persuade her grandparents to let her keep the puppy. At least until Thursday, when Caleb had promised he'd help her find its owner.

In the distance, the bells from the Lutheran church on the outskirts of town tolled the four o'clock hour. Years before, the bells had rung at the top of every hour, but at some point there'd been a dustup from new residents in the area. They had complained about noise pollution and said the bells were forcing religion upon everyone within listening range.

The Amish community had quietly supported their Lutheran friends in the disagreement. The bells were a long tradition, and there was a practical aspect to them too. Most Amish wore a wristwatch or carried a pocket watch, but not everyone did. And even those who lived in the strictest districts sometimes needed another way to track the hour.

In the end, the Birdsong Falls council decided that the bells would chime at eight in the morning, noon, four in the afternoon, and eight in the evening. Neither the no-more-bells group nor the bells-every-hour group had been pleased. Tally's grandfather had joked that the compromise must be a good one since neither group got what they wanted.

Maybe that's what she needed now—a compromise. One that would allow her to keep the puppy until she found either its owner or a suitable home for it. But what could she give up in the negotiation?

The resounding echo of the bell's fourth clang faded away. Tally tidied up the stall and patted the gelding's neck. She'd dallied in the barn long enough. At least the delay had provided her time to give Sprout a thorough brushing. But she couldn't postpone the inevitable any longer.

Tally leaned over the box and lightly stroked the fur of the sleeping puppy. If she volunteered to do the evening chores, Grossdaddi might not discover him until the morning. It was a good, sensible plan, except for the hammering of guilt against her conscience. Such deceit might allow her to put off telling them what had happened in town, but it would only cause her more trouble once they discovered the truth. Better to address the situation now.

After she'd pulled on her gloves, she poured the uneaten dog food back in the bag and carried it and the puppy box to the house. She entered through the rear door, into the mudroom. The spacious area contained a generator that operated a freezer, the washer and dryer, and the kitchen appliances. Shelves, cubbies, and hooks on the walls held winter coats, gloves, hand tools, cleaning supplies, and other assorted household items.

"Is that you, Tally?" Her grandmother's voice sounded muffled through the closed door that separated the mudroom from the kitchen.

"I'll be right in." Tally set the box down near the generator and put the dog food on a shelf. The puppy, apparently exhausted after the day's excitement, was still asleep. She stuffed her gloves into her pockets and hung her coat on the hook next to her grandfather's. Surprisingly, she felt relieved that he was home. Facing her grandparents together, and telling her story only once, was more appealing than reliving the entire embarrassing episode twice. And getting a double dose of disapproval.

Still, she knew that walking in carrying Scamp probably wasn't the best approach. She gave the sleeping dog one more glance, then opened the door to the kitchen and closed it softly behind her. Grossdaddi sat at the table reading a copy of *The Diary*, the monthly correspondence paper that published reports from Amish communities throughout the United States and Canada. Grossmammi stood at the kitchen sink, peeling potatoes. The warm scents of freshly baked bread and roasting meat filled the room, teasing Tally's taste buds and causing her stomach to grumble.

"You're finally home," Grossmammi said. "What did Mrs. Collins think of your poinsettias?"

"She loved them." Tally eyed the jar of homegrown green beans that stood on the counter. They were from the batch she'd helped her grandmother put up last summer. "Do you want me to fix the beans?"

"It's too soon for that. But these need to be chopped and added to the roast." Grossmammi pointed to three shiny orange carrots, already washed and peeled, sticking out of a colander.

Tally carried the carrots and a chopping board to the table and sat across from Grossdaddi. He lowered his paper. "Do I need to tend to Sprout?"

"All done." Tally sliced the first carrot into slanted pieces. "Fed, watered, and brushed."

"He's probably glad to be home after standing around town most of the afternoon. You kept him out of the wind, didn't you?"

"Of course I did." This wasn't a conversation she'd expected to be having. Grossdaddi knew that she was always mindful of Sprout. Ever since she was a *Kinner*, he had stressed the importance of taking proper care of the animals. Though he believed each one needed to serve a purpose on the farm in order to stay, he also provided top-notch care to his livestock.

"You're a *gut* girl. A horse isn't the same as a car, even if they share a purpose."

A strange peace suddenly bolstered Tally's spirit. Grossdaddi wouldn't be happy to see the puppy, she knew, but neither would he kick him out of the house. Especially not on a cold, snowy night.

"I'd rather have Sprout than the grandest car in the world," she said.

"If only everyone felt the same way about animals." He flipped the paper around and pushed it toward her. He jabbed a finger at one of the columns. "When I read something like this, I have to remind myself that we are a people of peace and forgiveness."

"Now, Aaron," Grossmammi gently admonished him. "Let's not have any of that kind of talk."

Tally skimmed the brief article about a community member in Indiana whose horse had been seriously injured by a gang of rock-throwing adolescents. So that was why Grossdaddi had questioned her about Sprout. Tally didn't like to think that it had taken something bad happening somewhere to create an opportunity for good. But given the circumstances, the article—and Grossdaddi's mood—did seem like a minor miracle.

"This is horrible," Tally said. "How could anyone let something like this happen?"

"Bad things happen every day," Grossmammi said. "We are blessed to know so little of what happens in the world of the Englisch. I, for one, wouldn't mind knowing even less."

"Sometimes I agree with you, Iris. But not on a day when our Tally has been to town. What news do you have for us?"

The direct question took Tally by surprise. She stared at Grossdaddi, trying to read in his deep-set eyes whether he had already heard about the broken poinsettias, the puppy rescue, and the online news article. But she didn't detect any guile in his expression. Besides, manipulation wasn't Grossdaddi's way. Grossmammi, maybe. Grossdaddi, though, would tell her what he knew, if he did indeed know something. He'd also expect an explanation.

"Something unusual did happen." While she spoke, she cut the ends off the carrots. "A puppy almost got hit by a car right outside the florist shop. And a little girl tried to run into the street after him."

"It's a dangerous world out there," Grossmammi intoned. "I don't know why you enjoy going to that place."

"Now, Iris," Grossdaddi said. "Seems to me we should be giving thanks that those were *almost* happenings." He returned to reading his paper. "They had nothing to do with Tally."

This was the moment she'd dreaded. "Except that I saw the little girl pull away from her mother. And when I saw the puppy in the street . . . I didn't even think about what I was doing."

Grossdaddi laid down his paper again. His gaze held Tally's. "What exactly did you do?"

"I ran into the street to get him before—"

Grossmammi's gasp interrupted her. Perhaps that was just as well. Tally wasn't sure how she would have finished the sentence. *Before he got run over?* Saying that would have only alarmed her grandparents more.

Grossmammi came to the table carrying a partially peeled potato in one hand and the paring knife in the other. Her hands were shaking. "You weren't hurt?" As she took in Tally's appearance, the concern in her voice changed from fear to confusion. "That's not your dress."

"My clothes got muddy. Eliza let me borrow a dress and apron."

"Eliza went to town with you?"

"No." Tally shook her head. "I stopped in to see her on the way back."

"Instead of coming straight home?" Grossmammi pressed her lips together, accentuating the fine lines around her mouth. "If your own dress wasn't suitable enough for wearing, then it certainly wasn't suitable for visiting. I certainly hope Eliza's parents didn't see you."

"They weren't there." A yip sounded from the mudroom, and Tally's nerves went on full alert. Thankfully her grandparents didn't seem to have heard the high-pitched whimper. "I dropped a box of the poinsettias when I ran into the street," she said hurriedly. She spoke loudly, hoping to cover up any additional puppy noises for at least a moment or two more. "The pots broke."

"I hope Mrs. Collins wasn't too upset," Grossdaddi said. He'd picked up his paper again, and Tally got the sense he was only half listening. "How will you make it up to her? We must keep good relations with the Englisch as best we can. Especially when they're such *gut* friends of yours."

"Humph." Grossmammi turned back to the sink. "I'm not sure those flowers bring in enough money, considering all the time and trouble they take. That woman profits off your hard work."

Tally didn't bother correcting this misconception. She'd tried before, but her grandmother wasn't interested in facts. Grossmammi seemed to resent anything—and any person—who took Tally away from the farm.

"I'll take more plants to her in a couple of days," Tally told her grandfather. At just that moment, another whimper, a louder whimper, sounded from the porch.

A sharp bark followed. Grossdaddi lowered his paper, a bewildered expression on his face. He opened his mouth to speak, and Tally pushed back her chair, scraping the legs on the hardwood floor.

"Something else happened," she blurted. Her grandmother, who didn't seem to have heard the dog, faced her again. Grossmammi's tense shoulders and drawn face showed that her patience was definitely wearing thin. Tally's words tumbled over each other as she hurried to get them out. "I slipped on the sidewalk and fell. People took pictures. And the newspaper put one on their website. It was all an accident, and I didn't mean for it to happen. But it did and—"

The bark turned into a pitiful howl. Both grandparents turned toward the door that separated the kitchen from the mudroom.

"You brought a dog home?" Grossmammi asked Tally.

Tally imagined Nicole would have rolled her eyes if one of her parents had asked her such a ridiculously obvious question. Eye-rolling was not something Tally dared to do.

"I had no choice," Tally said in a pleading tone. "He couldn't stay with the Collinses. Mr. Collins is allergic. And the Schwartzes have refused to allow Sadie to have a dog after their last one died. Remember how upset they all were when that happened? What was I supposed to do?"

"Not make a spectacle of yourself, for one thing," Grossmammi retorted. But the hardness in her voice was offset by a flicker of something in her eyes. Something akin to fear, Tally thought. But why would Grossmammi be afraid? She seemed to sense Tally's keen attention. "Return it to whoever it belongs to," she snapped.

"Nobody claimed him in town," Tally protested. "Besides, he won't be here long. Caleb promised to help me find his owner. We're going to the newspaper office on Thursday. Maybe the puppy's owner will see the photograph they published and contact them."

Tally noticed that sweat had begun to bead on her grand-mother's forehead. Grossmammi gripped the table as if to keep herself from falling to the floor. Tally wasn't sure whether to go to her or stay put. The expression in Grossdaddi's eyes told her he, too, was struggling with something that Tally didn't understand. Finally, he rose from the table. To Tally's surprise, he strode past his wife and walked into the mudroom. Through the now-open door, he murmured quiet words too low for Tally to hear. A moment later he appeared in the doorway with the whimpering puppy cradled in one arm.

"Could he be hungry?" he asked.

"I gave him food when we were in the barn, but he seemed too sleepy to eat."

"I don't think he's too sleepy now," Grossdaddi said. "Feed him again before his cries get any louder."

Tally exchanged a tense glance with her grandmother. Grossmammi released an exasperated sigh, then she began to attack another potato with the knife. She acted as if the dizzy spell, or whatever had come over her, had never happened. "He eats in the mudroom," Grossmammi said.

Tally wiped her hands on her apron and took Scamp from her grandfather. He smiled and placed his hand on her shoulder. "You were not hurt when you fell?"

"Only a little. I'm fine now."

"That's *gut*." He gave her a little push through the mudroom door and closed it after her. A clear signal that he wanted to talk to her grandmother in private.

Tally found a chipped bowl in a cupboard and scooped the kibble into it. Then she sat on the cold floor, her skirt wrapped around her stockinged legs, while Scamp devoured the food.

At least Grossdaddi seemed to understand that she'd had no choice but to bring the little furball home. Now that he was here, what could her grandparents do about it? They both had strict standards for her, but neither one was coldhearted enough to toss the puppy out the door into a bitter winter night. Tally only wished that their charity wasn't weighted with gloomy tension. "Maybe I should bring my dinner out here and eat with you." She scratched Scamp behind the ears. "I think you'd be better company this evening."

The comparison game usually wasn't one she enjoyed playing. She'd observed enough of human behavior, both within the Amish community and among the Englisch, to know that wishing for the impossible only brought discontentment. She was also mature enough to know that no one was immune from problems. Not even the Collinses.

Still, she allowed herself to indulge in the game while the puppy finished his supper. Sharing a pleasant mood while eating felt nourishing to her, and the mealtimes she'd shared with Nicole's family fed her soul as much as her stomach. At the Collins house, good humor regularly accompanied the good food, and Tally always felt honored to help clean up afterward. Clearing the table and loading the dishwasher were two small ways she could return the favor of being invited to sit at their table.

"If not for Mr. Collins's allergies, you could have stayed with them." Then Tally giggled. "I think I'm glad he has allergies! Is that wrong of me, do you suppose? It's only because I like having you here with me."

She glanced toward the closed door. The murmur of voices rose and fell on the other side. "Though I'm sorry to have upset Grossmammi. And I'm sorry this can't be your home."

Scamp licked the bowl clean and then climbed into Tally's lap. He placed his front paws on her chest and caught the dangling strings of her Kapp with his tiny white teeth. She laughed at his playful antics and then held him close while he licked her chin.

"I wish I never had to give you up," she whispered. A futile wish, and yet a fervent one.

Tally and her grandparents reached a compromise over supper. That is, her grandparents said that Scamp could spend his days in the barn and nights in the mudroom until Tally found either his owner or a new home.

To Tally's relief, nothing was said about her photograph appearing on the newspaper's website. Was it possible her grandparents had been too distracted by the strange noises coming from the mudroom to have heard that part of her story? She hadn't mentioned the photo again, and her guilt over this gnawed at her, especially after they told her Scamp could stay. She didn't want to be dishonest, but neither did she want to risk another upset. At least she could honestly say that she *had* told them—she couldn't help it if they hadn't heard her.

Later that night, when Scamp wouldn't settle down to sleep in his box, Grossmammi surprised Tally, and warmed her heart, by wrapping a hot water bottle in a towel and placing it next to the puppy. She dismissed Tally's wonder at the helpful trick by saying she'd read about it somewhere and that they should all hope it worked if they wanted to get any sleep.

That had been earlier in the evening. Now Tally was dressed in a long flannel gown and snuggled beneath the covers in her narrow bed. Her bedroom, one of three rooms located on the house's second story, faced south. From its window she could see anyone who passed by on the paved road that bordered the Byler farm. Or who turned into the drive leading to her home.

On nights like tonight, when a chill wind swept around the corners, she was grateful for the cocoon of warmth Grossmammi's hand-stitched quilts provided. The quilts Tally had made were stored in the trunk at the foot of her bed along with woven pot holders and embroidered pillowcases, sheets, and towels. This assortment of linens, along with a few other gathered items, would stay there until it was time for her to make a home of her own. Not that she was in any rush. Although she chafed under her grandparents' rules, she also understood that the days of her youth were limited. Once she was married, she could never have these days back again. So she treasured them—even the complicated, up-and-down ones like today when she'd been humiliated in public, pampered by Nicole and Mrs. Collins, labeled a heroine by the local paper, and also enjoyed moments of tranquility with her friends.

And when she couldn't put it off any longer, she had also faced her grandparents. Though they'd reacted as she'd expected, they still had also managed to surprise her—Grossdaddi by cradling Scamp in his arms and Grossmammi by comforting the pup with her warm water bottle trick.

Tally hoped that the warmth from the bottle would help Scamp sleep through the night. Her grandparents' bedroom was on the first floor. Any whimpering or barking would disturb them. Tally feared that if that happened, they might insist on him spending his nights in the barn, too, and not just his days.

It occurred to her now that if Scamp slept in her bedroom, then *she'd* be the one awakened by any noises. As long as she put him back in the mudroom before her grandparents got up in the morning, she told herself, they'd never know.

She dismissed this idea immediately. Who was she kidding? They'd know.

At the very least, though, she could check on him. Besides, she was thirsty. She'd just go downstairs, get a drink of water, and listen at the mudroom door to be sure he was asleep.

Ignoring the twinge to her conscience, Tally slipped from her bed and pulled on a robe. She tiptoed down the stairs, careful to step over the creaky board on the third step. When she reached the bottom, she paused to listen for any unusual sounds.

Were those voices?

As she neared the kitchen doorway, the voices grew louder. Why, she wondered, were her grandparents still up this late?

"I heard what she said," Tally heard Grossmammi saying. "Her photograph is on a website. I don't know much about such things, but I know that can't be good."

"I don't suppose it is," Grossdaddi replied. "Though I doubt most people care about our small-town newspaper."

"Perhaps we should go away for a while. Other folks go on trips. Deacon Fisher took his family to Florida last winter. They could tell us the proper place to go and how best to arrange such a journey."

A trip? Tally pressed her back against the wall. In all her years, they'd never traveled farther south than Baltimore. And she'd been there only twice. Why did her grandparents want to go away now?

"Tally said other people took photographs too." The anxiety in Grossmammi's voice was almost palpable. "All these mobile telephones are nothing but a nuisance. Why do they all need to have cameras on them? It's ridiculous the way the Englisch are always taking pictures. Of themselves and whatever else they want."

"You're fretting too much about something that is not in our hands," Grossdaddi said. "The good Lord will not allow those pictures to be seen by those who should not see them. We must believe that."

"I would prefer for *no one* to see them. Tally is no longer a Kinner. She should know better than to draw such attention to herself."

"That was not her intention. Her kind heart led her to rescue this puppy without giving any thought to her own safety. We shouldn't be surprised that the newspaper wanted to share such a story."

"What if she'd been—"

"She wasn't," Grossdaddi interrupted. "For that we can be thankful."

"Yes." Grossmammi's voice was so low, Tally had to strain to hear her. "But I am thankful only for that. Not for the story and not for that creature."

Grossdaddi chuckled. "This creature has kept me up too late. He doesn't care that I have cows to milk before the sun comes up."

"Go on to bed, then. I'll stay up with him."

Grossdaddi didn't answer, but Tally imagined that he probably looked as surprised as she felt to hear Grossmammi's surprising offer.

"Hand him over," Grossmammi continued. "I'll only toss and turn if I go to bed now."

"All right, then." A chair scraped against the floor, and muffled footsteps rounded the table. "Here you are."

Tally wanted to peek around the doorframe, to see with her own eyes whether her grandmother was actually taking the puppy. Perhaps Tally should volunteer to do so herself. She only needed to step into the kitchen. But then they would know that she had been eavesdropping—a transgression neither grandparent would easily forgive.

"Don't stay up too late, Iris. Morning comes early for you too."

"I won't. Go on with you now."

Tally scurried up the stairs to the landing as noiselessly as she could. She peered between the banister railings as Grossdaddi made his way to the fireplace stove, added a log to the burning pile inside, and then disappeared into his bedroom.

On her way back to her own room, the words Tally had overheard echoed in her mind.

"Perhaps we should go away for a while."

"The good Lord will not allow those pictures to be seen by those who should not see them."

But why should they go away? Who was it that shouldn't see the photographs?

Her grandparents were the only ones who could answer those questions, but Tally didn't dare ask either of them for an explanation. She'd only get in trouble, and her curiosity wouldn't be satisfied. The only blessing that had come from her unintentional snooping—and it definitely was a blessing—was learning that Grossmammi didn't despise Scamp as much as she pretended that she did.

Maybe, just maybe, Tally thought, she would be able to keep him after all.

CHAPTER FOUR

Cradling Scamp in her arms, Tally hesitated outside the door to the newspaper office. She'd walked past the two-story brick building before, but she'd never been inside. The printing on the plate glass windows on both sides of the door read:

The Birdsong Banner
Birdsong Falls, Pennsylvania
Established 1825

Tally hefted Scamp up higher in her arms and tightened her hold on him.

"Don't you want to go in?" Caleb asked.

"No. Yes." Tally lowered her head and breathed in the sweet smell of puppy goodness. She'd brushed Scamp that morning, despite her grandmother's grumbling that she was wasting time on something that wasn't worth doing. But Tally had continued the task secure in the knowledge that Grossmammi didn't regard the puppy with as much disdain as she wanted Tally to believe. She longed to know how long her grandmother had stayed up with Scamp that first night. But if she asked, then she'd have to admit to eavesdropping.

She had other questions too. About this supposed trip Grossmammi was proposing. About her grandmother's fearfulness. But none of them felt like questions she could ask.

"Tally?" Caleb's voice broke into her thoughts. "If you'd like, we could go to Birdie's Café for lunch and come back here later. My treat."

The offer was tempting, but practical concerns overruled her heart. She doubted she could take Scamp into the diner with her, and there was no sense in postponing what had to be done. If someone was missing this little boy, she was only adding to their heartache with each minute she delayed his return.

"I'm ready to go in." She forced a smile and took a deep breath.

"They're only people," Caleb said. "A little different than us, but still the same."

How like him to understand that there was more to her hesitation than her reluctance to give up the puppy. With the exception of the Collins family and a few other Englisch friends, Tally tried her best to avoid the townspeople and the tourists who flocked to the area. She admired the ease Caleb showed while interacting with strangers. He didn't seem to distrust others the way her grandparents did. It was a distrust she seemed to have inherited.

"You'll explain why we're here?" she asked.

"If you wish for me to."

"I do."

Caleb nodded, then pulled open the door. Tally preceded him into the bright interior. Though dark wood paneling covered the walls, widely spaced overhead lights and floor lamps dispelled any shadows. An old printing press stood against a wall under an array of historic newspaper editions displayed in frames. The moon landing. President Kennedy's assassination. The bicentennial of Birdsong Falls.

A long counter separated the lobby area from the receptionist's desk. An older woman with a pert haircut smiled at them as they approached.

"I recognize you," she said to Tally. "And that adorable puppy." The receptionist's pleasant expression helped Tally feel more at ease, and she swallowed the lump that had threatened to choke her. Caleb was right—this woman was different from them, but she was also the same.

"Did you get a chance to see your latest photo on our website?" the woman asked.

"Latest?" Tally blinked at the woman. "You posted more than one?"

"There've been so many to choose from. It seems everyone who has one wants us to print it. Let me show you." The receptionist pointed a remote toward a wall monitor that was currently tuned to a cable news channel. The screen immediately switched to a display of the newspaper's home page. A moment later, Tally's photo filled the screen. In this one, Scamp was nestled in Tally's arms as she maneuvered her way from the street toward the sidewalk.

"I've lived here in Birdsong Falls all my life," the woman said, an apologetic note in her voice, "so I know you Amish don't like to have your photos taken. But the story was too big to ignore. You're a hero for saving that little fur baby. Could I hold him?"

Tally lifted Scamp across the counter, her cheeks warmed by the woman's effusive praise. She still didn't think of herself as a hero. If Caleb had been there that day, he would have rescued the puppy. In the same circumstances, Eliza would have done the same, though she'd have fretted and fussed for days afterward about having become so muddied. Even Nicole, who cared about the state of her shoes more than Tally did, would have rushed into the street.

"We came to see if anyone recognized him," Caleb said. "Surely someone who saw the photo knows who he belongs to."

"Not that I know of." The woman swayed from side to side as if she were rocking a baby instead of a dog. "I wish I could take him, but we already have three of our own. Mr. Harvey might kick me to the curb if I brought him home. Though he sure is a sweetheart, aren't you, you little snookums?" When she scratched under his chin, he tried to catch her fingers with his tiny paws.

A middle-aged man with salt-and-pepper hair and sleeves rolled up to his elbows emerged from an interior door and walked toward them. He greeted Tally and Caleb with a curious smile and then noticed Scamp. "What have you got there, Irene? Is that the pup who almost caused a multicar pileup over on Birch Street? What a story that would have been. Glad it didn't happen."

"Me too," Mrs. Harvey said. "My poor heart couldn't take that much excitement." She turned to Tally and Caleb and introduced herself. "And this here is Mr. Edmond. He's the chief editor of the *Birdsong Banner*."

"Glad to make your acquaintance." Mr. Edmond reached across the counter to shake hands with Caleb and then nodded at Tally. "That was a brave thing you did. I hope you're not too upset about your photographs being posted. I take full responsibility for that decision."

"I don't mind," Tally said. Though she hardly dared to admit it even to herself, both photos she'd seen had pleased her. Dawdling in front of a mirror was a sin, she knew, but was it a sin to acknowledge that the photos depicted an attractive girl? Grossmammi probably thought so. She'd quote Proverbs 31:30 to Tally, reminding her, "Favour is deceitful, and beauty is vain . . ."

Caleb cleared his throat. "We stopped in to see if anyone called about the puppy."

A frown flickered across Mr. Edmond's face. "Someone did this morning, but of course, I couldn't give him your name," he said to Tally. "The person who gave us the photos didn't know it, and since he isn't a professional photographer, he didn't have you sign a release." Mr. Edmond scratched the back of his head. "In fact, you'd be doing me a favor if you'd sign one now. I'd like to put the story in the weekend edition."

Tally exchanged a quick glance with Caleb. Caleb shrugged his shoulders.

Mrs. Harvey stepped closer to the counter. "There's nothing nefarious going on, I promise. The release is a simple document that says you give us permission to use your image."

"Isn't it a little late for that?" Caleb asked.

"Like Mr. Edmond said, we didn't know who . . . I'm sorry, honey, what's your name?"

"Tally Byler. I mean Talitha. Talitha Byler." Could she not even say her own name in front of these strangers without stumbling over her tongue? "Please, call me Tally. And this is Caleb Schwartz."

"I must say, it's good to meet both of you." Keeping Scamp tucked in one arm, Mrs. Harvey opened a file drawer and removed a sheet of paper. "This is the release our regular freelance photographers give to their models. Take your time reading it over. We're not in any hurry here."

Tally took the document and held it between her and Caleb so he could read it along with her. It seemed fairly straightforward. There was nothing she could do about the photographs that had already been posted. She supposed she could ask for them to be taken down, but she didn't want to do that. Though it seemed somehow wrong to admit it, as if she were taking undue pride in her appearance, a part of her was enjoying the unexpected attention.

She snuck another glance at her image, still up on the wall. The photograph alone seemed to tell a story. She told herself she would admire it just as much, probably even more, if another Amish girl were its subject. At least, she wanted to believe that was true.

"We can offer remuneration if that would persuade you to sign," Mr. Edmond said.

"You'll pay her?" Caleb seemed as surprised by the offer as Tally.

"It's not standard practice," Mr. Edmond replied, "but I could make an exception."

"That's not necessary." Tally skimmed the document one more time. "I'll sign it."

"Appreciate that." Mr. Edmond handed her a pen, and she quickly signed on the appropriate line.

"You said you had a phone call from someone," Tally reminded him once she was done.

Mr. Edmond frowned again. "So I did. Though I can't say for sure he owns this pup, he seemed adamant it was one of his. There's no proving it one way or the other, of course."

Tally wasn't sure what to make of Mr. Edmond's reluctance to give her the man's name. Would he consider her rude if she simply asked him for the information? The Englisch rules of etiquette could be difficult to understand at times. Nicole had laughed when Tally had once made that observation, but then she had agreed.

"My goodness, Bill," Mrs. Harvey said. "Who in the world are you talking about?"

Mr. Edmond flashed her an annoyed look. "It was Oscar Wray."

Irene's mouth formed an O, then she grimaced. "What did you tell him?"

"The truth. That I didn't know who had the puppy." He shot a glance at Tally and Caleb. "Oscar raises dogs out at his place. Sometimes people file a complaint with the local humane society, but no allegations of neglect have ever been proven. The sheriff investigates, but when he goes out there, the kennels are clean and the dogs appear healthy."

"I doubt it's healthy for them to live their lives in cages." Mrs. Harvey seemed to tighten her hold on Scamp. "The ones that don't get sold, I mean. If people stopped buying his puppies, then he wouldn't keep breeding them."

"Why do they?" Caleb asked. "Buy his puppies, I mean."

"Folks who know better don't," Mrs. Harvey said. "But he's got a website with lots of fancy photographs on it. People click on a puppy, type in their credit card number, and wait for their new dog to arrive on their doorstep. Not much different than buying a book or a pack of toilet paper."

"I think the process might be a little more involved than that." Mr. Edmond's tone suggested he doubted his own words. "I can give you his number if you'd like. You can use our phone to call him."

Tally wasn't sure whether to accept the offer. She'd helped Nicole out at the florist shop often enough to feel comfortable taking orders over the phone. But that wasn't the same as talking to a strange man whom both Mr. Edmond and Mrs. Harvey obviously disliked.

"Do you have his address?" Caleb asked.

"I can look it up." Mr. Edmond pulled a dilapidated telephone directory from a desk drawer. He grinned as he plopped it onto the counter. "This may be the last phone book in town."

"I wouldn't be so sure," Caleb said with a smile. "My grandparents still have one even though they've never had a telephone."

"Is that so?" Mr. Edmond appeared amused as he flipped the pages. "I find what I need faster in here, and it's better than always getting on the computer. It's amazing how often it comes in handy despite being years out of date. Oscar will be listed in here, though. He's lived out on that farm of his since he was born."

He ran his finger down the page. "Here it is. Oscar Wray." He scribbled the address on a scratch pad and handed it to Caleb. "Do you need directions? Irene can print them out for you."

Caleb read the address, then slipped it in his pocket. "That will be helpful, *Ja*."

"Guess I better give this little man back to you." Mrs. Harvey gave Scamp one last hug and handed him to Tally. He licked Tally's fingers, and as she pulled him close, she caught a whiff of his puppy breath.

How, she wondered, could she return him to someone who would keep him in a cage? And yet what choice did she have? None at all if he actually belonged to this Oscar Wray. She almost wished she hadn't been the one to rescue the puppy when he ran into the street. Then she wouldn't have to face the pain of saying goodbye to him now.

⁓

If Caleb had known how long it would take to get to the Wray farm, he might have hired someone to drive them in a car. There were several Englisch in the town who provided transportation services.

On the other hand, Caleb enjoyed having Tally next to him on the seat. Her cheeks were pink from the chilly weather, though, and he imagined her toes were cold, despite her sturdy boots. The puppy, wrapped in an old blanket, lay nestled in her lap.

"This might be it." Tally gestured toward the mailbox at the end of a curving drive. The faded gold letters affixed to the side of the mailbox might have once spelled *Wray*, however, the *r* and the *a* were missing now.

At the other end of the slush-covered lane stood a two-story farmhouse in need of a fresh coat of paint. Two rusted vehicles mounted on concrete blocks stood near a dilapidated shed that didn't appear sturdy enough to withstand a strong wind, and other outbuildings in various states of disrepair flanked the house.

Caleb directed Buttermilk to make the turn. His palomino mare took dainty steps, testing the rutted ground beneath the layers of slush, as she pulled the buggy toward the house. Caleb let her take her time. Now that they were here, he found that he wasn't in a hurry to meet this Oscar Wray. Tally's firm grip on the puppy showed him that she wasn't either.

As they neared the house, two long-legged mongrels with shrill barks raced toward them. Caleb pulled back on the reins, bringing Buttermilk to a halt, and then hopped from the buggy. The mare snorted a warning at the dogs, and Caleb slipped his fingers around her bridle. The dogs stopped several feet away, barking and growling. Caleb pretended to pay them no mind while keeping a close eye on them.

Caleb glanced toward Tally. Her focus was on the farmhouse. He followed her gaze as a man with an uneven gait came toward them. Caleb raised a hand in greeting, but the man only yelled a brusque warning at the two dogs. They stopped barking and scurried toward him, their tails tucked beneath their legs.

"Do I know you?" the man shouted as he shortened the distance between them. He wore a corduroy jacket over a stained shirt and gray sweatpants tucked into rubber boots. A knitted stocking cap covered his head. His salt-and-pepper beard framed a pockmarked face that looked like it had at one time been used as a punching bag. He definitely had been in a few brawls in his time.

"Are you Oscar Wray?" Caleb asked.

The man halted several feet away and gave him a long, appraising look. "Depends who's asking."

"I'm Caleb Schwartz." Caleb started to introduce Tally but then changed his mind. Oscar Wray didn't need to know her name.

"What's your business here, Caleb Schwartz?" The man's attention shifted to Tally, who'd stayed in the buggy.

"Mr. Edmond at the *Birdsong Banner* gave us your name and address," Caleb continued. "He said you'd called—"

"You're the gal who rescued my pup." Wray stepped closer to the buggy. "I saw your picture on the paper's website. You got him up there in that contraption?"

"We do," Caleb answered. A strange tingling crept up his spine, and he caught Tally's gaze. Her eyes pleaded with him to do something. She didn't have to say anything for him to know she didn't feel comfortable returning Scamp to this slovenly man who seemed to care so little about his appearance or surroundings.

"How did you happen to lose him?" Though Caleb's tone remained pleasant and nonaccusatory, Wray glared at him.

"I don't see that's any of your business. Now just hand over that pup, and you can be on your way. I don't care much for strangers on my property."

Caleb exchanged another quick glance with Tally before facing Wray again. Her stoic expression gave little away, but the misery in her eyes pained his heart. Only Gött knew what would happen to Scamp after they left. Would he go to a good home? Or would he live the rest of his life in a cage?

There was only one way to be sure. He could end Tally's misery by purchasing the puppy. Though her grandparents probably wouldn't appreciate the gesture, Tally would be delighted to have Scamp as her own. He straightened his shoulders. In this instance, he was willing to ask Aaron Byler for forgiveness instead of permission. Hopefully, the older man wouldn't hold the bold move against him later if . . . when . . . Caleb and Tally married.

He gave Wray a broad smile. "Mr. Edmond told us that you're in the puppy-selling business. How much are you asking for this one?"

Wray's eyes narrowed to an intimidating slit. Despite his unease, Caleb managed to appear relaxed. He hated for Tally to be in such close proximity to Wray. Part of him wanted to grab the puppy from her, hand it over to the unkempt man, and hightail it out of there. But he knew he'd never be able to live with himself if he didn't try to save the puppy from an unknown fate. Tally had rescued Scamp once. Now it was Caleb's turn.

"That there pup's a designer breed," he said with obvious pride. "An Aussiedoodle, he's called. The sire is an Australian shepherd, and the dam is a poodle. Dogs like him don't come cheap, and they aren't meant to be farm dogs. They're used to luxury."

"So you raise them in your house?" Caleb asked.

Ignoring the question, Wray feigned a good-humored grunt and gestured toward Tally. "Thanks to your girlfriend there, his value's gone up some. Why, he's a local celebrity now."

Caleb inwardly bristled at the man's casual reference to Tally as his girlfriend. The Englisch term didn't begin to express the feelings he had for Tally or the hopes he had for their future together. Sensing that Wray was purposely trying to get a reaction from him, however, he forced himself to maintain a placid expression. Besides, what else could he do? The man appeared to be an experienced brawler. Caleb had never hit anyone in his life and had no plans to ever do so.

"How much?" he asked again.

"Starting price is a thousand dollars."

Behind Caleb, Tally let out an audible gasp. "A thousand . . ."

"I suppose I owe you something for making sure he didn't get turned into a pancake," Wray continued. "I might could agree to eight hundred. You got eight hundred to spend on a luxury pet?"

Caleb understood that Wray was trying to bait him and that he needed to remain calm. He blew out a long breath and avoided turning toward Tally. He should never have gotten her hopes up by asking about the price.

He hated disappointing her, but he knew she'd never expect him to spend that much money for any dog. Both his parents and her grandparents would be shocked if they knew he was having this conversation with Wray. Even one hundred dollars would seem outrageous to them when puppies could be found cheap, or even free, at the farmers' market.

"That's an impossible price," he said.

"I don't run no charity, no matter how grateful I am to you for bringing him back. Guess I'll take him, then." Wray started toward the buggy, but Caleb stepped in front of him, and Wray backed off.

Caleb turned to Tally, who gave him a weak smile. "I'm sorry," he said too softly for Wray to hear.

"I know." She gave Scamp a hug, then reluctantly handed him to Caleb. "Please. Let's go quickly."

Caleb nodded as he scratched the tan fur beneath Scamp's chin. The expression on Wray's round face—smarmy, Caleb thought—riled his insides even more. Words spilled from his mouth almost before he'd thought them. "I'll give you two hundred. Cash."

"Caleb," Tally exclaimed. "You can't."

He ignored her, staring at Wray as if daring him to refuse. Caleb hated the idea of doing business with this man—of giving him any of his own hard-earned money. But he hated the idea of leaving Scamp with him even more.

Wray stared back for a moment, then shook his head. "There's expenses to raising a litter of pups, especially ones as fine as these. Hand me eight hundred or my property. Your choice."

Defeated by the man's greed, Caleb slowly held out the puppy.

Wray took him in one meaty hand, and Scamp yelped. "Now, now, don't be doing that," Wray grumbled as he tucked the puppy beneath his jacket. "Don't want these fine folks to think I don't take care of what belongs to me, now do we?"

Caleb couldn't stomach any more. He climbed into the buggy, leaving only a few proper inches between him and Tally. He needed to be near her wholesomeness. He hoped it would chase away the stink of Wray's foul coarseness. He wanted to believe she needed him too. He couldn't give her Scamp, but—for whatever it was worth—he could give her comfort.

Wray didn't wait for Caleb to turn the buggy around. He strode toward a squat outbuilding. On its front door was a sign that read Dynamic Doodles. The two lanky mongrels, their tails wagging, followed close behind him.

Wray's destination answered Caleb's question about whether the puppies were being raised inside the house.

The ride back to town was a long and quiet one. When they reached the main road, snow began to fall in gentle flakes from the sky, as if attempting to draw their attention to the beauty of Gött's creation and away from the ugliness achieved by slovenly men.

CHAPTER FIVE

Relief washed over Tally when she saw that her grandparents weren't home. Caleb started to climb down from the buggy once they got to the Byler place, but she stopped him. They hadn't said much to each other on the long drive back through town to their side of the county. The lump in her throat had made it difficult to talk, and she was afraid that sharing a lingering goodbye now might cause her to fall apart in front of him.

Her sadness over leaving the puppy with Oscar Wray wasn't the only reason for the tears she was barely holding back. Caleb's kindness and generosity had touched a deep place inside of her heart.

She'd always had a roof over her head, plenty of food to eat, and clean clothes to wear. Her grandparents provided her with a good and comfortable home. But though each of them had secretly cared for the puppy, neither of them would have ever thought to purchase him for her. That Caleb had offered to pay two hundred dollars for Scamp still astounded her. She could think of no other man in their community who would do such a thing—nor could she think of one who wouldn't consider Caleb foolish for having done so.

Even though Mr. Wray hadn't accepted the money, Tally would never forget Caleb's sweet gesture. They weren't technically courting, but—especially now—it was clear to her how much regard he must have for her. How much *love*.

If . . . when . . . he asked her to be his wife, she would say yes with no hesitation.

While she waited for her grandparents' return, Tally got a head start on supper. Not knowing when they'd be home, she decided to make a pot of chili. She retrieved a jar of homemade tomato sauce from the basement pantry and poured it into a saucepan. As the sauce heated, she cut up onions, tomatoes, and both red and green peppers. Once the diced vegetables were added to the sauce, she browned ground beef in a large iron skillet. She also sliced chunks of sausage and added them straight to the sauce.

When she heard the buggy coming up the drive, Tally turned up the heat on the simmering chili and put a skillet of cornbread in the oven. She was just placing cloth napkins next to the plates on the kitchen table when her grandparents entered the house carrying canvas bags filled with paper goods and a few staples.

"How long have you been home?" Grossmammi set her bags on the counter. There was a hint of annoyance in her tone.

"Less than an hour." While the cornbread baked, Tally helped put away the groceries. Since Grossmammi didn't ask about Scamp, Tally didn't mention him either. She'd relived the trip to Oscar Wray's farm over and over again in hopes of finding a reason to believe that the puppy was in good hands. Instead, she'd only become more dejected.

"Do I smell chili?" Grossdaddi asked as he came back into the room after checking the livestock. "That's a welcome supper for a cold day like today. It warms the insides and provides nourishment too. Danki, child."

After the cornbread was out of the oven, Tally added pats of butter to the top and brushed the melting liquid over the golden warmth. Grossmammi ladled the chili into deep bowls. Once they'd gathered around the table, Grossdaddi said grace.

No one was very talkative, but Tally didn't mind. Both of her grandparents seemed on edge, even Grossdaddi, who'd praised her chili. They were probably waiting for her to bring up the subject that weighed on all their minds. She didn't think of herself as being obstinate, but the former ache in her stomach now felt like a stone. If her grandparents wanted to know what happened to Scamp, they'd have to ask.

When they'd finished eating, Tally rose to clear the table. Grossdaddi laid his hand on her arm. "Sit down for a spell. The dishes can wait awhile longer."

Tally stood beside her chair. "I did what you asked. There's nothing more to say."

"You found the owner, then?" Grossmammi asked.

"Ja, we did." Tally heard her voice shake unexpectedly. She took a deep breath. "I can clean the kitchen on my own."

"Sit down, Tally," Grossdaddi said again as he patted the table. "Today has not been the finest for any of us."

Unwilling to disobey her grandfather a second time, she reluctantly returned to her seat.

"Several of our neighbors talked to us when we were in town. Including Deacon Fisher," he continued. A knot formed in Tally's stomach. She considered the deacon's son Marcus Fisher to be a *gut* friend with a quick wit and ready laugh. He and Eliza often attended community events with her and Caleb. But his father's piercing eyes and stern demeanor intimidated her.

"They all know about your picture." Grossmammi pushed away her plate and folded her hands. "It's disgraceful what that newspaper did."

Tally lowered her eyes. This definitely wasn't the time to tell her grandparents about the release she'd signed. Or about the fact that Mr. Edmond planned to publish her photograph in the newspaper's Sunday edition. They'd find out soon enough, once the paper was delivered to the farm.

On second thought, she realized, she probably should tell them before then. But she'd let them have their say first.

"I told Deacon Fisher that you and Caleb were going to the newspaper office today." Grossdaddi paused, waiting for Tally to respond. "Did you?"

"We did." She traced the ivy pattern on the tablecloth with her finger. No use in waiting any longer. "Mr. Edmond, the editor, apologized for posting the photograph. He took full responsibility for making the decision to post it. He said Scamp's rescue was major news in the community."

Her grandparents exchanged a look with each other. "That isn't a good enough reason," Grossdaddi said. "He knows our ways. Knows that we do not wish to be on display."

"Especially a young girl such as yourself," Grossmammi added. "It was thoughtless of him."

Tally inwardly bristled at her grandmother's description of her as a "young girl." She was nineteen—no longer a Youngie, except in Grossmammi's eyes. Tally had wanted to take the baptism classes when they were held last fall, but Grossdaddi had discouraged her from doing so. Until she did that, she couldn't join the church or marry. He'd given her no reason for the delay but had simply asked her to wait. Once again, she had done what her grandparents wanted, without question. But his failure to explain, and the sense that they were hiding something from her, grated against her spirit.

Now she was having to defend the actions of an Englischer, a stranger who'd been nothing but polite to her, to her grandmother.

"I found him to be kind," Tally said. "And good-hearted. He . . ." She paused and bit her lip. *He offered to pay me.* Another secret to keep to herself. Even though she'd refused the money, her grandparents might consider the offer an insult instead of a goodwill gesture. She didn't want to give them any more reasons to be upset with the editor. Not when Oscar Wray should be the object of their contempt.

"He what?" Grossdaddi asked.

"He told us where to find the puppy's owner. Mrs. Harvey— she was at the front counter—printed the directions for us."

"So you did return the puppy." Grossmammi gave a quiet sigh of relief and rose and gathered the chili bowls.

"I already told you I did." Tally had aimed for a respectful tone, but her words were sharper than she intended. She braced herself for another reprimand. Instead, she was surprised by Grossmammi's response.

"So you did," she said quietly, almost as if she were speaking to herself. She wiped her forehead with a cloth napkin and then stared at Tally. "It's over and done with, then. We need discuss it no longer."

"He's not a kind man." The words escaped Tally's lips without her giving them any thought. Grossmammi had been reaching across the table to stack the plates. Her hands paused in midair and then fell to her sides.

"*Who* isn't?" Grossmammi sounded as if she dreaded hearing the answer to a question that she couldn't help but ask.

"His name is Oscar Wray. He raises what he calls designer breeds and sells them on the internet. He said Scamp was an Aussiedoodle, part Australian shepherd and part poodle." Tally looked from one grandparent to the other. Both of them were giving her their full attention. She took a deep breath. "There are rumors that Mr. Wray doesn't take proper care of his dogs. But nothing is ever done to stop him. At least that's what Mr. Edmond said."

"Did you talk to this Oscar Wray?" Grossdaddi's voice was full of concern.

"Caleb did. I stayed in the buggy."

"I'm glad of it." Grossdaddi drew his coffee mug close as he relaxed in his chair. "Caleb is a good man. A sensible man."

"*Caleb* offered to buy the puppy." Tally regretted the words—and her tone—as soon as she uttered them. What was wrong with her that she couldn't have a civil conversation with her family?

Grossmammi stared at her, a shocked expression in her eyes. Grossdaddi recovered from his surprise more quickly.

He glanced toward the mudroom, then back at Tally. "But you didn't bring him home?"

"Mr. Wray asked too much. More than Caleb could pay."

"That puppy wasn't worth more than a few dollars." Grossmammi scoffed. "Leave it to an Englischer to think otherwise."

"He wanted a *thousand.*" Tally pushed away her feelings of guilt. It felt strangely satisfying to show her grandmother that she didn't know as much as she thought she did about the world outside of their community. "He said he'd take eight hundred, but Caleb only had two hundred. It wasn't enough."

Grossmammi stared while Grossdaddi practically choked on the sip of coffee he'd just taken.

"Caleb offered the man two hundred dollars? For that puppy?" Grossdaddi was incredulous. "He wouldn't have."

"I'm not lying."

"No, of course, you're not." Grossdaddi immediately sounded apologetic, not that he'd ever say he was sorry. "But that's a ridiculous amount of money to pay for any dog."

"Caleb must not have thought so."

Grossmammi resumed stacking the dishes and carried them to the sink. She kept her back to them as she spoke. "It's been a long day. Go on to your room, Tally. I'll take care of things in here."

"I can help." Tally put the lid on the butter dish as she rose from her chair. It was difficult for her to say *I'm sorry* too. Perhaps helping with the cleanup would ease her guilt over the way she'd spoken.

Grossdaddi gently took the butter dish from her. "Do as you're told, child," he urged, his voice sympathetic. "You've done your share by fixing us a fine supper. It does a man good to open his door to the delicious smell of chili on the stove. I'll give Grossmammi a hand if she needs one."

Tally walked out of the kitchen, but instead of going to her room, she settled in a corner of the sofa. She removed her shoes and sat sideways, her arms tucked together along the sofa back as she stared through the front window into the dark shadows of the night. Though Scamp had only been with them such a short time, his absence inexplicably pained her. She missed him. She worried about him.

But what could she do except pray that whoever bought him from the horrible Mr. Wray would give him a good and loving home? She could pray the prayer, but she'd never know God's answer. That thought only made her sadder. If only there was something more she could do.

The murmur of voices from the kitchen caught her attention. She couldn't make out the words, but the urgency of the tones, the rhythms of the sounds, indicated that her grandparents were arguing. Truly arguing.

How odd. These two people rarely had a cross word to say to each other.

Tally wondered if her impulsiveness had somehow led to this fracture in her family. She felt sure that she'd done nothing wrong by saving Scamp, yet her world had since turned so topsy-turvy that she hardly knew which end was up. Her emotions were in a turmoil. Anger and sorrow had stirred up an uncharacteristic feeling of spitefulness against her grandparents. All of these feelings had overshadowed her deep regard for the one person who seemed to understand things about her that she didn't even understand herself. Danki Gött for Caleb. Danki Gött that he cared for her as much as he did.

She hoped he would realize how much he meant to her when he saw her Christmas gift to him. Before today, she'd worried that her present—one that she had thought of and which Nicole was helping her obtain—might seem too personal. Perhaps even too intimate. But after what he'd done for her today, she no longer harbored those concerns.

The voices from the kitchen grew louder, then softer. Unable to bear the arguing any longer, Tally walked toward the door with the intention of interrupting. But the sound of her grandmother's words through the door stopped her.

"We should leave. Pack up as much as we can and go before anything else happens."

"This is our home, Iris. We don't need to abandon it."

"But what if—"

"That won't happen."

During the pause that followed, Tally cracked the door open and peered into the kitchen. There, she saw her grandfather cradling her grandmother in his arms. Grossmammi had her hands over her eyes, and her shoulders were shaking.

"We'll go to Florida," Grossdaddi said. "Like you wanted. And then, when this situation with Tally is no longer on everyone's minds, we can come back. You'll see. Something else will happen to cause tongues to wag and our neighbors to scold. Meanwhile, we'll be walking on sand instead of through snow. You'd like that, wouldn't you?"

Grossmammi nodded. "We should leave soon. Before anything happens."

"I have to make arrangements for the farm. We'll go early next week. I promise."

Grossmammi lowered her hands. Tears slid down her wrinkled cheeks as she slipped her arms around Grossdaddi. "I only want Tally to be safe."

"I know."

Tally stepped away from the door, careful not to make a sound, then hurried up the stairs and plopped onto her bed. She replayed the conversation in her mind, but it still made no sense to her. Why would Grossmammi want to leave her home, their community, because of a silly photograph? To keep Tally safe, she'd said. But safe from what? The only danger Tally could foresee was the lecture she'd surely get when the Sunday edition of the *Birdsong Banner* came out.

The sound of the back door opening and closing drew her attention. Grossdaddi was probably headed to the barn to make his final check on the animals before bedtime. Perhaps she should join him and ask why Grossmammi was so desperate to leave.

But instead of moving from her bed, she slipped beneath the covers, even though she hadn't changed into her nightgown or brushed her hair.

Her grandparents had a secret. She'd always known that. But she'd been raised from toddlerhood to pretend she didn't— trained to ignore the odd snippets of conversation and occasional hints about their past. The secret that had remained buried for so long now seemed close to being uncovered. But Tally couldn't bring herself to be the one to do it. She wanted to know what her grandparents were hiding from her. At the same time, the secret felt like a monster waiting to destroy her.

Perhaps it was best for the monster to stay hidden. Best to ignore its presence, just as she'd done her whole life.

Why seek out trouble when trouble could only cause harm?

CHAPTER SIX

As soon as Tally arrived with more poinsettias for the florist shop, Nicole excitedly ushered her into the break room. Her expression resembled that worn by the Cheshire cat from *Alice in Wonderland*. Though Tally had never read the classic children's story, she'd seen an animated version of it while spending an afternoon with Nicole when they were younger.

Tally had hoped she might talk to Nicole in private about the unsettling conversation she'd overheard the night before. Even more unsettling was the fact her grandparents had behaved this morning as if their disagreement had never happened. Tally supposed Grossmammi was satisfied with Grossdaddi's plan. But neither grandparent mentioned the Florida trip to Tally. What were they planning to do? Wait until it was time to board the train to tell her?

Nicole, however, had her own news to share. She placed a tote-box filled with envelopes and packages on the table. "All these are for you."

"For me?" Tally selected one of the smaller packages. It was addressed to "the Amish girl" in care of the florist shop. The other envelopes were marked similarly. She didn't recognize any of the return addresses. "I don't understand. Who are these people?"

"They're your fans, and they're sending you presents because you're an internet sensation." Nicole shook one of the boxes. "Isn't it great? I can hardly believe it myself, but it's true."

"I'm a what?"

"An honest-to-goodness, true-life *internet sensation*." Nicole grabbed her electronic tablet off the table and tapped a few buttons. "Look at this. Everyone's sharing your photos. There's even a hashtag, #AmishAngel."

"I'm not an angel." Tally's voice sputtered. "That's a blasphemous thing for people to say about me."

"They don't mean a literal angel, silly." Nicole wasn't at all concerned about the propriety of theological semantics. Her dismissal of Tally's concern, however, did nothing to ease Tally's discomfort at being the center of a scandal. "They mean that you're Scamp's guardian angel because you saved him from certain death."

"All I did was—"

"Risk your life to save his. Like it or not, you're an angel. Besides, look at the image that's getting the most attention."

Nicole turned the tablet around so Tally could see the photo. Tally pressed her hands against her burning cheeks. "Oh! What will my grandparents say about that?"

"They'll say they have a brave and beautiful granddaughter." Nicole's flippant attitude only deepened Tally's feeling of impending doom. "It's an attractive photo. Everyone thinks so. Besides, what are the chances they'll ever see it?"

"I hope they never do." Tally took the tablet from Nicole and stared at the photograph. If her grandparents ever saw this particular photo, they might decide they needed to do more than take a trip to Florida . . . they might choose to move there permanently.

At least she had been standing in the photographs the newspaper posted on their website. In this photo, clearly taken just after she'd fallen, her head rested on the sidewalk and was surrounded by bright red poinsettia leaves. Scamp—that dear, sweet puppy with his gray-mottled coat, tan markings, and white chest—nestled against her neck.

Tally scrolled through a few of the comments below the photo, her embarrassment growing stronger with each one she read.

Such a pretty girl. What's her name?
Great photograph!!! Who's the model?
Aw! I want a puppy like that one!!!!

"This can't be happening." Tally handed the tablet back to Nicole and tried to unjumble her thoughts. The photograph *was* flattering, and that admission made her feel both pleased and guilty. Unlike Nicole, who loved to primp in front of a mirror, Tally had been taught that focusing on one's outer appearance led to pride. And that pride led to sin.

Yet the photo clearly did make her appear attractive. Perhaps the photographer had touched it up with one of those filters. She knew about those, too, from spending time with Nicole.

"Enjoy the attention while it lasts. I'm a little jealous I wasn't the one who rescued that puppy." Nicole suddenly frowned. "Where is he? You could have brought him with you. Daddy won't be here today."

Tally's throat suddenly felt dry. She fingered the loose edge of a strip of tape on one narrow, oblong box on the table. The return address was a post office box in Chattanooga, Tennessee. She'd never been to Chattanooga, knew no one who lived there, and doubted she could find it on a map. Yet someone in that city, the same person who'd wrapped this box with a wide strip of packaging tape, knew her. As did all these other people who'd sent her boxes and envelopes.

They thought she'd done something wonderful. What would they think if they knew she'd given Scamp back to the person who'd lost him in the first place? A person who saw only dollar signs and not an adorable puppy?

"What's wrong, Tally?" Nicole asked. "If you're that worried about your grandparents, then ask my mom to talk to them. She can tell them that none of this is your fault."

"It's not just that." Tally absentmindedly tugged at the tape, but it remained stuck beneath a second strip of tape that crossed over it. "I found out who Scamp belongs to."

"Oh, I'm glad." Relief flooded Nicole's voice, but at Tally's pained expression, she gave her friend a closer look. "Or maybe I'm not. Who is it?"

"Do you know someone named Oscar Wray?"

"I don't think so."

Tally focused on peeling the edge of the cross-tape from the box. Though mildly curious about the contents, she wasn't focused on opening the box. Fidgeting with the tape simply helped steady her. "He sells puppies. For lots of money."

"What's wrong with that?" The unexpected defensiveness in Nicole's tone stilled Tally's fingers. "I have an aunt who raises Pomeranians. The puppies are very expensive, but so are the screenings, the vet care, and everything else she does to ensure they're healthy and well adjusted. She gets rave reviews from her buyers." Nicole tapped the keys on her tablet. "Here's her website. Aren't they the cutest little things?"

Tally smiled at the photos of the tiny black Pomeranians. As she took a closer look, she noted something interesting. "She raises them inside her house?"

"Where else would she raise them?" Nicole laughed. "In a barn?"

"Mr. Wray does." Tally pictured the squat building. "Technically it's not a barn. More like an outbuilding. Think how cold they must be. How lonely."

Nicole closed her tablet and set it aside. "Oh, Tally. I wish we could have taken Scamp."

Tally wished that too. Though, once she'd found out whom he belonged to, she couldn't have given him to anyone else without being guilty of theft. "Mr. Edmond, the editor at the *Birdsong Banner*, said there have been complaints about the kennels. But nothing ever happens to Mr. Wray."

"Do you think the complaints were valid?" Nicole asked. "Did you go into the building?"

"I didn't even get out of the buggy. Thankfully, Caleb was with me. Mr. Wray made it very obvious he didn't want us there."

Nicole touched Tally's arm. "Maybe the building is heated. He may not take the same care my aunt does, but he's not going to let his puppies freeze to death. Then he'd have none to sell and no money."

"Maybe you're right," Tally agreed, though she still had her doubts. Mr. Wray's place wasn't the only homestead in Lancaster County that was in need of a makeover. So was the farmhouse that Caleb was renovating. But an older house in need of work could still be neat and tidy.

To Tally's mind, the junk and debris at Mr. Wray's farm showed he didn't care about his place. She doubted he cared enough about the puppies to get them the kind of quality health screenings that Nicole's aunt gave her litters. Little Scamp wasn't the only one being raised in harsh surroundings.

"I'll pray that a wonderful family buys Scamp," Nicole said. "God will take care of him."

"I'm praying for that too. I'll never know the answer, though."

"But God will."

After a few moments of heavy silence, Nicole's expression suddenly brightened. "I almost forgot. Caleb's book is finished. It'll be here tomorrow."

For the first time in days, Tally's spirit rose. In her concern over Scamp and over her grandparents' strange behavior, she'd thought only fleetingly about the special Christmas present she'd ordered for Caleb. For several weeks, she and Eliza had secretly gathered the poems Caleb had written for them and other family members. Nicole had located a printing company in Philadelphia that published what they called legacy books. Most were limited print runs of family genealogies or collections of stories.

With Nicole's help, Tally had ordered one copy of Caleb's carefully organized poetry. This was her special Christmas gift: returning to him the poems he'd given to her and his family over the years. Poems that said what was in his heart—his appreciation for simple joys and poignant moments, his respect for the land and for tradition, his love for his community. Even a few that seemingly conveyed unspoken feelings for her.

"That's great news," Tally exclaimed. "I can't wait to see it."

"I can bring it to your place after it arrives."

Tally thought a moment, then shook her head. Though her grandparents were always polite to Nicole, they weren't as welcoming to her as Mrs. Collins was to Tally. Besides, if her grandparents were still upset at that time, Tally might welcome an excuse to get away from the farm. "I'll come get it. Danki for all your help."

"That's what friends are for."

"Caleb will like the book." Tally searched Nicole's face. "Won't he?"

"He'll love it." Nicole gave her a reassuring smile. "He's so talented. More people should be given the chance to read his poetry."

"I feel the same. But I don't think Caleb would agree. He rarely shows his poetry to anyone outside of his family."

"He's overly modest, in my opinion. But I suppose that's the Amish way."

"So it is." Tally returned to picking at the tape on the narrow, oblong box.

"Do the Amish no longer use scissors?"

Tally looked at her with a dazed expression.

"Cut the tape and open the box," Nicole urged, her tone both excited and impatient. "I want to see your presents."

The first package contained a leather dog collar and matching leash. A perfect and thoughtful gift, if only she still had Scamp. The accompanying note mentioned the #AmishAngel photo. Tally put the gift and the note back into the box. "I can't keep this." She gestured at the other packages. "I can't keep any of these."

"Aren't you curious to see what's in them?" Nicole asked. "I am."

"You open one."

Nicole eagerly selected a package from Barre, Vermont. Inside was a tin of maple sugar candy and a box of assorted chocolates. She clasped her hands in delight, her eyes wide. "You'll keep these, won't you? Please!"

Tally couldn't help but laugh at Nicole's over-the-top plea. "I shouldn't."

"Look at this note. It was written with a crayon and signed, 'Love, your friend, Lauren, age 6.' And she likes 'your pretty bonnet.'" Nicole clutched the note to her chest. "This is too adorable. Oh, Tally. You can't send this one back. You'll break little Lauren's heart."

"I wouldn't want to do that now, would I?"

"Absolutely not. Now open that tin. I love maple sugar candy."

"You open it." Tally traded the tin for the note, which was decorated with flowers and hearts. After reading Lauren's sweet message, Tally folded the note and placed it in the box. She'd need Lauren's return address to send a thank-you card.

While sampling the delicious candy, Tally and Nicole opened the other packages. Most contained puppy-related items—another dog collar, a variety of toys, a doggy coat and boots. The enclosed notes usually contained a photo of the sender's dog.

But others contained jewelry, cologne, and fragrant lotions—items that were totally inappropriate for strangers to send an Amish girl who was old enough for courting. Tally agreed to keep another box containing candy, but no one should have sent her a beaded bracelet, a silver chain with a snowflake pendant, body spray, or scented body wash.

Everything but the candy had to go back. She made sure the return address label remained intact as each box was opened, and she placed each gift back in the appropriate box.

"What about the letters?" Nicole asked. "Don't you want to open them?"

"I will later." The presents had been overwhelming enough. Tally's heart had ached each time she opened a gift meant for Scamp. And she didn't even want to think about the more personal gifts meant for her. Hopefully, most of the letters would be from sweet six-year-olds like Lauren. "It's getting late and I have chores."

As Tally pulled on her coat and gloves, Nicole placed the boxes and letters back in the tote-box. "Don't forget to come back tomorrow," she said. "I have classes in the morning, but after that I'll be home." Besides working at the florist shop, Nicole was a student at a nearby community college.

"I'll be here," Tally assured her. Holding Caleb's book of poetry in her hands would be the bright spot in what had turned out to be a dark week. One that could get darker still if her grandparents followed through with their ridiculous travel plans.

"I only want Tally to be safe." Grossmammi's strained words echoed in Tally's mind. They made no more sense to her now than they had when she first heard them. She'd intended to tell Nicole

about the conversation, but the opening of the gifts and the news of Caleb's book had pushed that intention aside. Maybe they could talk about it tomorrow. Or maybe the conversation she'd overheard was one she should keep to herself.

Nicole would only ask the same question Tally had—safe from what? And Tally didn't know the answer.

Perhaps she never would.

CHAPTER SEVEN

Caleb removed the crown molding from the miter box and placed it on the top bar of the potting table he was making for Tally for Christmas. But the newly created piece didn't fit the adjoining one. He'd placed the molding backward in the miter box. How had he made such a stupid and novice mistake? He hadn't done anything so foolish since he was a Kinner.

He tossed the molding aside and leaned against the doorframe of his outbuilding. From this vantage point, he could see beyond his farmhouse and its adjacent land to the fields his parents had given to him when he joined the church last year. A few months later, the previous owners of this property, which bordered his parents' place, had decided to move to Virginia to be closer to their grandchildren. When he'd heard about the Kellers' intentions, Caleb had snatched the place up before anyone else had a chance.

The combined land was now his, and someday the house would be his home. He and his future wife would raise their children here. In his mind's eye, he could almost see the family he'd have one day. The boys, building a snow fort near the barbed wire fence that enclosed the pasture. The girls, making angels on the snow-covered lawn between the house and the graveled lane. His wife, standing on the porch, a knitted shawl wrapped around her shoulders as she called the Kinna to their supper. Her face was the easiest one to picture.

Tally.

This outbuilding would be hers and hers alone. Once he'd finished expanding it, it would be part nursery, part shed, and part greenhouse. A place where she could nurture and grow her flowers and plants. A place where—if she needed to—she could go to escape the demands of motherhood. Even escape him, if she had the mind to do so. Caleb chuckled, remembering the advice his father had given Jonah, his firstborn son, before he married. *"A woman needs a spot to call her own, where she can be left alone."*

Jonah had built his bride a gazebo. And before Caleb's other brother, Daniel, married, he'd transformed a small shed into a cozy quilting retreat.

Caleb's plans were more ambitious. Perhaps too ambitious, considering that he planned to add a greenhouse to the existing structure before next summer. But he could already imagine Tally's delight the first time she laid eyes on the renovations he was currently making. Until he was done, he was keeping her out of the outbuilding.

With the potential of such a bright future ahead of him, his strange feeling of foreboding seemed out of place. He sauntered toward the house and, ignoring the cold, settled onto the weathered porch swing. The rusted chains creaked beneath his weight, but he trusted that they'd hold.

He pulled a small notebook and a pencil stub from his pocket and scoured the landscape in search of inspiration. Writing often soothed his spirit when he felt uneasy, but today his mind was too scattered to settle on a single image or a pertinent phrase. Individual words flitted through his mind, but they didn't fit together except in trite formations that he discarded as quickly as they formed.

Something was bothering him. He had to admit that truth and figure out what was causing unease. Or, more precisely, who. *Tally.*

Her initial reaction to the photo that Irene Harvey had displayed on the monitor at the newspaper office was what he would have expected. Embarrassment. Even a misplaced sense of guilt, though she'd done nothing wrong. But then the blush of embarrassment had somehow changed to the sort of pleasurable blush that followed an unexpected compliment. The exact hue that sometimes rose to her cheeks when *he* complimented her. She should have been mortified by the attention the photo was receiving, Caleb felt, instead of being drawn to it.

Though perhaps he was being unfair. He had to admit that the photograph was attractive. That Tally was attractive. The photographer, an amateur with a phone at the ready, had captured Tally in a moment when nothing mattered to her except Scamp's protection. Her Kapp and a cuddly puppy only added to the feeling of innocence the photo conveyed. No wonder the editor had wanted the photograph to appear in his newspaper.

But Tally had signed that release with barely a moment's hesitation. Though she'd held the document so he could read it with her, she hadn't asked his advice on whether she should sign it. She'd simply ignored the offer of payment and signed her name, as if sharing her photograph with the Englisch world was a common occurrence.

Caleb stabbed the notebook with the pencil point, breaking the lead. It suddenly occurred to him that Nicole was the source of the problem. Tally wouldn't even have known that the first photo was on the *Banner*'s website if Nicole hadn't told her. Caleb had always liked Nicole and her parents. They were good and fine folks. But Nicole's world was different than his and Tally's. He didn't usually mind the friendship between the two young women, but sometimes—like now—he wondered if it was too deep.

At the thought, he bowed his head. Such harsh thinking seemed all wrong and didn't reflect who he was or who he wanted to be. Their Amish community was separate from their Englisch neighbors. It always would be. But they were still neighbors, and they were still friends. He prayed that Gött would forgive him for believing, even for a second, that the Collinses were his enemies because of their regard and affection for Tally.

As he reflected further on the day, another thing became clear: his frustration wasn't with Nicole or with Tally. He was upset with himself because he'd been unable to give Tally what she wanted most—Scamp.

He'd surprised himself by offering Oscar Wray two hundred dollars for the puppy. If his father ever found out, he'd wonder if Caleb had been kicked in the head by a mule. The higher price Wray demanded would have been out of the question even if Caleb had possessed ten times, a hundred times, that amount.

Tally understood that. And yet her sad disappointment had wrapped around them throughout the long ride home. There had been nothing he could say or do to change the situation, and so he'd said nothing, done nothing, while each clop of Buttermilk's hooves pounded out the incessant echo of his failure.

Caleb tilted back his head and closed his eyes. The chill breeze gusted unevenly against his cheeks. The house offered protection to his left side while his right side was more exposed to the wind circling the porch.

A poem lived in that tension.

Protect. Expose.

Protect. His left side. His heart. A house. A home. Love.

Expose . . .

The positive word associations for one word whirled in his mind, but he couldn't do the same for the other. All he knew was that Tally belonged on the side of the swing between him and the house—protected from the harshness of life, near his heart, the heart of his home. But today, he'd failed her, and the poem struggling within him was gasping for breath.

Buttermilk's hooves. The incessant echo of his failure.

He rested his forearm across his closed eyes and listened for other sounds. But the clopping hooves in his imagination only grew louder. Closer. He opened his eyes and then waved as Daniel—his closest brother in age, older by only fourteen months—halted his buggy near the porch.

Daniel climbed up the rickety steps and perched on the railing. "So this is what you do when we think you're working on this place," he teased. "You'll end up living here alone if you don't do something about this house."

"You should have been here ten minutes ago," Caleb said. "Or maybe it's better that you weren't."

"Something wrong?"

"I made a mistake when I was working on Tally's potting table. That's why I'm taking a break."

Everyone in Caleb's family suspected his affection for Tally, but Daniel was the only one who knew that the reason for Caleb's slow progress on the house was the time he was spending on renovating the outbuilding. Weddings wouldn't take place again until after next year's fall harvest, though, so he still had many months to get the house ready for them to move into it. Assuming, of course, that the young lady he wished to court during those long months said yes.

"What kind of mistake?" Daniel asked.

When Caleb hesitated to answer, his brother laughed. "That bad?"

"More like that stupid. You don't want to know."

"Ja, I think I do."

Heat crept up Caleb's neck. If he told Daniel, the teasing would eventually end—most likely once Daniel did something equally ridiculous. Caleb heaved a huge sigh. "I cut the wrong slant on a strip of crown molding."

To Caleb's surprise, Daniel didn't laugh. Instead, he stared at Caleb and then motioned for him to scoot over so he could sit beside him. "I heard Tally rescued a dog that was trying to cross a busy street," Daniel said as he lowered himself to the swing. "I'm thinking there's more to that story."

Caleb silently gave thanks for his brother's intuitive thoughtfulness. Sitting side by side, they were able to talk quietly while staring at the horizon instead of each other. Not having to make eye contact made it easier for Caleb to open up about the confusion he'd been feeling. He told Daniel about his and Tally's visits to the newspaper office and to Oscar Wray's farm, about his impetuous offer to buy Scamp, and about the silent ride home.

Daniel asked a question here and there, but mostly he listened. Caleb finished with the story of how he'd accidentally placed the crown molding the wrong way in the miter box. After he was done, the brothers sat in silence. The porch swing chains creaked under their weight, and Daniel's horse occasionally grunted or sighed. The wind picked up, and the sun drew closer to the horizon.

"I think it's *gut* you didn't spend your money on the dog," Daniel finally said. "But if I were in your boots, I think . . . I hope . . . I would have made the same offer to comfort my Deborah."

Caleb darted a sideways glance at his brother. "Danki, Daniel. That eases my mind."

Daniel stood and started toward his buggy. When he reached the bottom porch step, he turned. "Remember the wisdom of our elders: 'A happy home is more than a roof over your head. It's a foundation under your feet.' Tally has been in your heart since we were Kinna. The foundation of all those years of care won't crack now unless you allow it."

Caleb let those words sink into his spirit as Daniel drove away. The proverb his brother had quoted was popular with courting couples. Caleb had seen embroidered renderings of the quote hanging on walls in a few of their neighbors' homes. But until this moment, he hadn't considered the idea that he and Tally had started building the foundation for a possible future home together years ago.

He wouldn't let that foundation crack now because of events that neither he nor Tally controlled. Besides, Scamp was gone now. Tongues would wag when Tally's photo appeared in the weekend edition of the *Banner*. But then days would go by and something else would occur that would take the attention away from her.

In the meantime, he had work to do. Christmas was coming, and his present for Tally wasn't nearly finished.

CHAPTER EIGHT

Tally added wood to the corner stove and then perched herself on the high stool in her workroom. Years ago, Grossdaddi had fixed up a storage area in the southeast corner of the barn for her to use as a makeshift nursery and potting station. The stove made it possible for her to spend time there even on cold wintry days and also provided needed warmth for her more delicate plants.

She spread a clean tarp on the workbench before her and laid the unopened envelopes on it. The letters had come from as far as Missouri and Texas to the west, and from as far north as Maine. Two were from Georgia. She opened a letter from Texas first.

When she unfolded the sheet of stationery, a check fluttered to the top of the workbench. Her heart thumped at the amount: one hundred dollars. With shaking hands, she read the accompanying letter. Its writer wished her a Merry Christmas and wanted to know what she'd named the puppy. The person called the money a small gift from one animal lover to another. Tally carefully replaced the letter and the check in the proper envelope and then opened the other letters. Almost all contained a check or cash. The total came to $950.

Despite her long friendship with the Collins family, Tally still didn't completely understand the Englisch ways. But these unexpected and unnecessary gifts went beyond even that incomprehension. Now she wished she'd opened the letters with Nicole. Maybe her friend could explain this strange generosity.

Several of the letter writers mentioned Tally's courage and bravery. If only they knew that what they called courage, her grandparents called foolhardiness and recklessness.

Tally's emotions were as complicated and mixed up as the contents of a wheelbarrow filled with potting soil, vermiculite, and peat moss. And just as impossible to separate into distinct elements. She felt stunned, flattered, and grateful, but also embarrassed by the attention.

Besides, almost all the letters asked her to buy something for the puppy or said that the money was meant to help provide for him. The puppy wasn't hers, so how could she accept the money? Should she pass it along to Mr. Wray? The idea made her shudder.

Unless . . . the thought burst forth, flowered, then quickly faded. Her grandparents had forced her to return the puppy before. They'd never allow her to buy him now. Especially not at the price Mr. Wray had set.

"That puppy wasn't worth more than a few dollars," Grossmammi had said. Nothing Tally said or did now would change her grandmother's mind.

Tally gathered the gifts and letters into the tote-box and took it to the house. For the moment, she left it inside the mudroom. She couldn't postpone the inevitable forever, but why ruin the rest of the afternoon? After supper, she'd show the mail to her grandparents and face the storm that was sure to follow. It seemed unfair that she should suffer backlash over something beyond her control. Yet receive it she would, and she'd do so while keeping her thoughts and feelings to herself. Like she always did.

Tally felt her body draw up taller and straighter, a sensation almost as if a steel rod were suddenly bolstering and straightening her spine. She'd always been obedient, yet that obedience hadn't yielded even the tiniest amount of trust from her grandparents. She'd worked hard, but that cheerful labor hadn't motivated them to offer her any understanding. Even during Tally's *Rumspringa* years, she'd been content to stay home, help with the farm chores, and tend to her flowers.

How had her grandparents thanked her? By turning her one heroic moment, her short time in a spotlight she hadn't even sought out, into an unseemly spectacle that apparently embarrassed them so deeply they now needed to leave the county. How did that make any sense? And why were they keeping their plans—plans that affected her—a secret?

Trust between the Bylers seemed as fragile as the icicle now hanging from an eave of the porch roof. One swift swipe, Tally imagined, and it would fall onto the paving stone below, shattering into irregular shards. Left alone, it would melt away, a constant drip, until nothing of it remained.

Both scenarios tore at Tally's heart. She remembered the momentary sensation of a rod bracing her spine. Maybe it was time for her to stand up for herself.

If she didn't, who would?

As soon as the last supper pan was dried and put away, Tally retrieved the tote-box from the back porch. Her grandparents were now settled in the front room. A respectable fire burned behind the metal doors of the wood-burning stove that was inserted into the fireplace. The stove's heat efficiently warmed much of the house. The fireplace's long hearth stretched from the kitchen door all the way to the house's exterior wall. An old-fashioned popcorn popper, still in perfect condition, hung beside wooden bellows on one side of the stove. Fireplace implements stood in a brass stand on the other side.

Grossdaddi relaxed in the upholstered recliner Tally and Grossmammi had given him on his birthday a few years ago. The chair had been a rare extravagance, and at the time Grossdaddi had made a show of grumbling about how much they must have spent on him. But Grossmammi, blushing as if she were a schoolgirl with a crush, had shushed him with a smile and a kiss on the cheek. The rare display of public affection had warmed Tally's heart.

Grossmammi now sat opposite him on the other side of a round table that held a huge kerosene lamp. As she slowly rocked back and forth, she worked on the afghan she was knitting to place in a Christmas box for a needy neighbor. The two of them formed a comfortable—and comforting—tableau this quiet winter evening. A quiet Tally knew she was about to break.

Grossdaddi raised his eyes from *Martyr's Mirror*, a book he was reading for the umpteenth time, to smile at her. "What do you have in the box, granddaughter? Another lost pet?"

As Grossmammi made a humph sound, Tally smiled at his good-natured jest. But she quickly grew serious as she settled on the hearth and placed the tote-box beside her. "It's mail."

"I collected our mail this afternoon," Grossmammi said. She looked confused. "We got a seed catalog and a pizza flyer."

"This mail was delivered to the Collins's florist shop." Tally took a deep breath. Part of her was drawing strength from the image of the steel rod. Another part of her felt as if she were skating on a pond whose thin layer of ice was cracking beneath her feet. "But it's all for me."

"Why would anyone send mail to you there?" Grossmammi's needles stopped clacking. "That's nonsense."

"Who are the letters from?" Grossdaddi asked.

Tally chose to answer her grandfather's question first. "From strangers who saw photos of me on the internet. Nicole said I 'went viral.' That means—"

"I know what it means," Grossdaddi said, his eyes narrowing with irritation. "I just never expected my granddaughter to be a part of any such thing."

Tally focused on keeping her voice low but firm. "That wasn't my intention. But I couldn't stop people from taking photos of me or posting them to their social media accounts. Some of the photos had the florist shop window in the background. That's probably why the letters and gifts were sent there."

"Gifts?" Grossmammi's voice rose to a high pitch. "What kinds of gifts?"

"A few things for the puppy." She glanced to her grandfather and shot him a wry grin. "And chocolates."

He nodded his well-established approval of chocolate, then cleared his throat when Grossmammi glared at him.

"But also jewelry. Cologne. Some of the letters contained money." Tally's voice faltered, but she took a quick breath and hurried on before her grandparents could respond. "I know I can't keep any of it. And I don't plan to. So please don't lecture me. All I did was save a lost puppy from getting hit by a car. And humiliate myself by falling. Everything else, all this"—she waved her hand at the box—"I'm not responsible for what other people, kind and generous people, decided to do."

Grossmammi pursed her lips, and her rocking grew faster as her knitting needles flew. Tally half expected to see smoke pour from her ears. But to her surprise, Tally suddenly recognized something else: her grandmother's agitation was a thin veneer for something that went much deeper. Grossmammi was angry, yes. But more than that, she was afraid. It was this fear, and not Tally's situation, that drove her anger.

Grossdaddi gave his wife a sideways glance. Then he lowered the footrest on the recliner and leaned toward Tally. "Have you read all the letters?"

"Ja."

"May I read them?"

"Of course you'll read them," Grossmammi said. "So will I."

Tally handed her grandfather the tote-box. "I have nothing to hide."

"Tomorrow you'll take them to the post office," Grossmammi said. "They'll know how to return them to where they belong." The pace of her rocking slowed, as did the flashing of her needles. She gave Grossdaddi a pointed look. "We all know what needs to be done."

"You're right, as usual." Grossdaddi held up the box of chocolates from the tote-box. His eyes twinkled. "Though I think it'd be permissible for Tally to keep one of the gifts."

Grossmammi opened her mouth, no doubt to object, but closed it again without saying a word. Grossdaddi gave the candy box to Tally. "Go on to your room now. It's going to take me a while to read through these."

"Don't you want a piece?" she asked.

"Maybe tomorrow. That is, if you don't gobble them all up tonight."

"I'll save you one." Tally looked at her grandmother, whose eyes were focused on her stitching. "I'll save you both one. Good night."

She paused at the foot of the staircase, out of sight from her grandparents. Would she hear them arguing again? But all she could hear was the crackling of the fire and the occasional squeak from Grossmammi's rocker. Tally climbed the steps, not knowing whether her conduct had been proper or disrespectful.

From her grandparents' reaction, she gathered that perhaps it had been a mixture of both.

But Grossmammi's final words gave her no peace. *"We all know what needs to be done."* She'd meant to hide her meaning from Tally, but because of her eavesdropping, Tally could guess at the words' intent. Her grandmother wanted to leave Birdsong Falls. And soon! But did she only want to spend a week or two in Florida? Or did she want to leave their home and never return? And why did they need to go at all?

That night, the unanswered questions swirled in Tally's dreams, disturbing her sleep. But by the time the sun arose on a new day, she had formulated a new plan. A risky plan.

CHAPTER NINE

To Tally's surprise, Grossmammi seemed in a better mood than Grossdaddi at breakfast the next morning. The tote-box, with the packages and letters neatly stacked inside, had been placed in an out-of-the-way spot on the kitchen counter.

"Did you eat all the chocolates?" Grossdaddi's teasing tone seemed to contain a false note, and the twinkle in his eyes wasn't as lively as it was when he was in a truly jovial mood.

"I only ate one." Tally handed him the candy box. "You can have the rest. As long as you share with Grossmammi."

"I'll save mine for after breakfast." Grossmammi set a platter of bacon and sausage on the table. "It'll be a nice treat on our way to Lancaster."

Tally's eyes widened. "We're going to Lancaster? Is someone driving us?" The buggy ride to the county seat could be a pleasant venture in nice weather but not on a day as bitter as this one.

"You have other responsibilities to tend to this morning." Grossdaddi added a dollop of cream to his coffee mug, lightening the strong black liquid to a caramel brown. "I called Reggie Brown this morning after I milked the cows. He's driving Grossmammi and me." Like many Amish farmers, Grossdaddi had a phone in the barn that he could use when necessary. Mr. Brown was a local handyman who earned extra money by driving his Amish neighbors on those rare occasions when they weren't able to travel by horse and buggy.

"Why are you going to Lancaster?" Tally asked.

"'Blessed are the curious, for they shall have adventures.' Now let's thank the good Lord for this bountiful breakfast." Grossdaddi quoted the Amish proverb as if it answered Tally's question when his response didn't do that at all. The truth was, she *might* have an adventure if she went with them. But she most assuredly would if she stayed home and went through with her plan. That plan, however, had nothing to do with curiosity.

After Grossdaddi's prayer, the conversation shifted to more typical morning topics—the frigid weather, how much milk the cows had given that morning, plans for a local quilting bee. Tally barely listened. Her grandparents obviously had made a monumental decision after she had gone to bed. But even though that decision affected her, she'd have to wait for them to let her in on their secret.

The frustration she hid seethed inside her and spoiled her appetite. Even so, she lacked the courage to confess that she'd overheard their conversation about leaving their home. Neither could she demand that they tell her why they were going to Lancaster. If she did either of those things, she'd have to face her own hypocrisy. After all, she had a secret agenda for the day too.

After her grandparents left in Mr. Brown's minivan, Tally removed the letters from the tote-box. On each envelope, she recorded the amount of money inside and noted whether the writer had sent a check or cash. Once she'd finished, she placed the checks and cash in a new envelope and stuck it in her drawstring bag. She hid the letters in her dresser drawer and wrote thank-you notes for the candy.

All she needed now was an accomplice. She'd do what needed to be done on her own if she had to, but she prayed that wouldn't be necessary. She would first try the Schwartz farm.

As Tally halted Sprout beside the cleared pathway from the drive to the house, Eliza and Sadie came out on the front porch to greet her.

"Have you come for Caleb?" Eliza shouted. Tally had never hidden her affection for Caleb from Eliza. Similarly, she was well aware of Eliza's affection for Marcus Fisher.

"I've come for you." Tally stepped down from the buggy and walked over to her friend.

"May I feed Sprout?" Sadie asked. "I have an apple I can give him."

"That'd be fine. Danki." As soon as Sadie was out of earshot, Tally turned to Eliza. "Would you mind going into town with me? I have a couple of errands, and I'd appreciate the company."

"Only if Sadie can come along too. I'm watching her." Eliza's shoulders sank. "Though perhaps we better not. She's been sniffling lately. I probably shouldn't have allowed her to even come outside. But you know Sadie."

"Couldn't Sadie stay here with Caleb?"

"Caleb is at the old Keller homestead." Eliza's eyes danced, and her voice took on a teasing tone. "I don't know why he spends so much time working on that old house. If he has plans for the future, he won't tell anyone what they are. I don't suppose he's said anything to you either."

"No, he hasn't." Though Tally hoped . . . and believed . . . one day he would. Her warm smile hid her disappointment that Eliza couldn't join her, but she didn't want to take Sadie where she was going. She was relieved that Eliza had been the one to nix the idea.

"I had best be going, then. Hopefully the weather will stay fine for the rest of the day."

"I think it will." Eliza squeezed Tally's arm. "Go find Caleb. Ask him to go with you. If anyone can persuade him to take a break from work, it's you."

"I'm not so sure about that. Ever since he bought that farm, it seems he thinks of nothing else." Tally gazed in the direction of the old farmhouse, though seeing it from where she stood was impossible due to the hills and the woods. "I haven't been in a while, though. As much time as he spends there, it must look different now."

"I haven't been there either." Eliza shivered in the cold. "Stop by later. Sadie and I are baking molasses cookies this morning."

"Sounds delicious. I will if I can."

After saying goodbye, Tally directed Sprout to the road leading to the old Keller farm. How long would it be before people started thinking of the homestead as Caleb's place or the Younger Schwartz farm? Or maybe . . . maybe even Caleb and Tally's place. Though perhaps that was wishful thinking. Despite all the time Caleb had spent working on the house, he hadn't invited Tally to see his progress since he'd installed the new roof some time ago.

Perhaps he was waiting till the work was finished so he could surprise her. Or perhaps he planned on sharing his renovated home with someone else. Though that seemed unlikely. Caleb had never driven anyone but her home after a church sing.

When Tally reached the old homestead, she reined Sprout to a stop at the bottom of the drive so she could get a good look at the property. She couldn't help making certain comparisons. Like Oscar Wray's house, this one needed a fresh coat of paint. It also needed repairs to the wraparound veranda and new shutters. In all honesty, of the two places, this house—at least from the outside—seemed to be in worse shape.

But no rusted-out vehicles or metal scraps or broken farm equipment littered the yard or the fields here. Come spring, there would be weeds to pull, flowers to plant, and other landscaping chores to tend to. This farm had the potential to be as well maintained and as inviting as any of the places that surrounded it. The Kellers' poor health had led to their home's decline, and their children, who lived out of state, had had no interest in putting money into repairs or renovations. They preferred a fast sale that would make the property someone else's problem.

What the Keller offspring had seen as a problem, however, Caleb saw as an opportunity. He had the youthful vigor and strong work ethic needed to transform the property into a profitable farm again. Caleb was a model of stewardship. It was one of the things Tally admired about him. Mr. Wray couldn't do anything about his age, Tally knew, but she was sure he could rid his yard of its debris if he wanted to do so.

She dreaded the thought of returning to his kennels. At the same time, she was eager to get there as soon as possible. She flicked the reins, guiding Sprout along the snow-covered drive so that her buggy wheels stayed in the tracks she assumed had been left by Caleb's buggy. The tracks disappeared into a barn situated behind the house, but Tally stopped Sprout beside the weathered porch. She shaded her eyes and peered up at the new roof. The old roof had developed several leaks, so replacing it was a job that had needed to be done before winter.

This past September, the local Amish families and a couple of their Englisch neighbors had gathered together early one morning to tackle the task. By evening the work had been done. Tally's grandfather had helped, even though Grossmammi had forbidden him from getting on the roof. He'd had to find other ways to contribute to the day's work, such as sawing lengths of wood to replace the rotting struts.

Tally had helped serve the noon meal and clean up afterward. It had been a festive day, a fun day. More than one person had given her knowing looks as if she and Caleb were privy to a secret. But there was no secret. At least not yet.

Tally stepped from the buggy and climbed the porch steps. When Caleb didn't answer the front door, she tried the handle. The door was locked, so she peered through the window. All was still inside. Perhaps Caleb was in the barn. She maneuvered her way through the snowdrifts. She found Caleb's buggy parked in the barn's alleyway. Buttermilk stood in one of the stalls, munching on hay.

"Caleb?" Tally called. "Are you in here?"

Nothing.

She walked toward the rear of the barn where a single door stood open. Stepping-stones led from the door to one of the outbuildings. She guessed that was where Caleb was working. But what could he possibly be doing? It seemed like the house, not an outbuilding, would be his first priority, and if not the house, then the barn.

"Caleb?" she called in a singsong voice before venturing into the snow. "Where are you?"

All remained quiet in the snow-covered world. Even the winter birds seemed to be hiding. Her only option was to follow his tracks to the outbuilding.

"Caleb?"

CHAPTER TEN

Caleb had awakened that morning with a renewed sense of purpose. The day before, Daniel's words about a happy home's foundation had echoed in his thoughts while he cut another strip of crown molding—at a perfect angle this time—and affixed it to the upper shelf of the potting table. They'd stayed with him on the buggy ride home yesterday and during evening chores. But as he was drifting off to sleep, something else Daniel had said pressed against him.

"If I were in your boots, I think . . . I hope . . . I would have made the same offer to comfort my Deborah."

He'd thanked his brother at the time for saying those words. Upon reflection, his appreciation went even deeper. Caleb hadn't expected anyone in his family or their district to understand why he'd done something so outlandish. But Daniel, married less than a year and already expecting his first child, understood how a man's heart could cause him to do the surprising, the unthinkable, for the woman he loved.

Caleb couldn't give Tally the puppy she wanted. But he would give her a house that she could in time transform into a home.

Even before then, he'd give her a place that she could call her own, where she could be left alone. A Christmas present from his heart.

As soon as his morning chores at his parents' home were finished, he'd hitched Buttermilk to the buggy and driven to the homestead. After adding a few final touches to the potting table, he had sanded the wood surfaces. He planned to add the first coat of varnish later that day.

"Caleb? Where are you?"

He cocked his head. Had he heard Tally calling his name, or had she so completely invaded his thoughts that he'd begun to imagine her voice?

"Caleb?"

He wasn't dreaming. Tally was here, at the farm. He couldn't tell her his plans. Worse, she was close to the outbuilding. He dropped the sandpaper in his hand and hurried to the door. Through a window in the door, he spotted her taking long, exaggerated strides to plant her feet in the footprints he'd made earlier. He grinned, thinking he'd never before seen anyone so awkward and yet so beautiful.

But beautiful or not, she couldn't come into the outbuilding. That would ruin his Christmas surprise for her.

He slipped through the door and closed it tightly behind him. Tally stopped as she stepped up to him, her boots widening the print left by one of his own. "There you are." Her cheerful voice warmed Caleb from the top of his head to the tips of his chilled toes. "I've been looking for you."

Caleb closed the gap between them. When he reached her, he tucked her arm in his and led her back to the barn. "What brings you all the way out here?" She glanced behind her to the outbuilding. "It's a cold day to be driving around the countryside," Caleb said to distract her. "Shouldn't you be home by the fire, spinning thread?"

Tally, as he expected, laughed at the joke. As he knew all too well, she'd never spun thread a day in her life. But one day last summer, when they'd been at the general store, a tourist had cornered Tally and asked her all kinds of questions about spinning wheels and making thread. When Tally said she didn't know how to spin, the woman became indignant. "Isn't that what you do all day?" she'd said. "Sit by the fire and spin thread?" She'd practically accused Tally of lying before stomping out of the store.

Tally had been embarrassed that others had witnessed the encounter and also angry at the woman's rude ignorance. As if Tally had nothing better to do with her life than fulfill this brash woman's ridiculous stereotype! To cajole her back into a good humor, Caleb had treated Tally to a double-scoop mint chocolate chip cone at a nearby ice cream stand. Since then, the line had become an inside joke between them.

"I'd definitely be warmer," she said. "But I need to go to town. I was hoping you'd go with me." She glanced again at the outbuilding. "That is, if you're not too busy."

Caleb escorted her into the barn, stopping beside Buttermilk to scratch the palomino's nose. The temptation of an afternoon with Tally was hard to resist. But he didn't have many opportunities to work on the outbuilding. If he didn't stick with his task, it might not be ready before Christmas.

"When Eliza told me you were here," Tally continued, "I expected to find you in the house." Her curiosity was clear, and Caleb wasn't sure how to respond. He didn't want her to suspect his secret project had anything to do with her. But neither could he lie.

"Why are you going to town?" He started to mention that she'd been there only a couple days before but stopped himself. There was no need to bring up the disastrous trip to Oscar Wray's farm.

Tally turned away from him and fiddled with the cuffs of her coat, as if she needed a moment to gather her words. Suddenly she smiled at him and shrugged. "God blesses in strange ways at times. Ways we'd never expect. You believe that, don't you?"

"Of course I do." The proof was standing in front of him, this girl whom he'd known for as long as he could remember. During those years, she'd grown from a gawky Kinner he'd found as annoying as a summer mosquito into a beautiful woman who'd captured his heart.

"I took more poinsettias to the florist shop yesterday. Something unexpected happened."

Caleb waited for her to continue, but she pulled in her lower lip as if she didn't know what to say.

"Something good I hope."

"Ja. Very good." She gripped the top rail of Buttermilk's stall. "People who saw my photo sent me mail. In care of the Bouquet Bliss."

Caleb wrinkled his forehead. "Why would they do that?"

"To thank me for saving Scamp. To be nice." Her brown eyes looked deeply into his, a silent plea for him to understand. To say yes to whatever she asked of him. "There was money inside some of the letters. Checks and cash."

Money? Strangers had sent her money? That didn't make sense.

"Don't you see? God answered our prayers. I have enough money to buy Scamp." Now her tone was overtly pleading. "To take him away from that awful place."

"You have eight hundred dollars?" His voice practically squeaked in disbelief.

"Even more than that." She stepped toward him. "The money was to get things for the puppy. Food and toys. They said so in their letters. Before I do that, I have to get *him*. Today. Before Mr. Wray sells him to someone else."

Caleb shifted toward Buttermilk, hiding his face behind the horse's long neck. His long-engrained sense of propriety warred within him. The Amish didn't take money from the Englisch except in exchange for goods and services. Charity took place only within the community. Yet Tally had accepted this outpouring of charity as a blessing from God. If she was right, and that was indeed what it was, he couldn't refuse her.

But what if she was wrong? He'd never known anyone to spend hundreds of dollars on a dog.

Though he and Tally weren't officially courting yet, they were on the verge of taking that step. He'd already assumed the role of her protector, as much as he could while she still lived under her grandfather's roof, by driving her to Oscar Wray's farm. Even at two hundred dollars, Scamp would be no bargain. Caleb doubted the so-called designer pup could earn his keep on a farm, which made an eight-hundred-dollar purchase even more foolhardy. Didn't he have a duty to dissuade Tally from such nonsense?

Daniel's words whispered in his ear. *"I think . . . I hope . . . I would have made the same offer to comfort my Deborah."* But while two hundred dollars was extravagant, eight hundred dollars was insane. Caleb doubted Daniel would have ever considered making such an offer—not even to comfort Deborah.

"I'm sure you're very busy." Tally's voice sounded small, her cheerful tone woven with a thread of hurt. "I shouldn't have bothered you."

He swallowed a heavy sigh and faced her. "Perhaps we could go tomorrow." He wasn't sure he wanted to go then either. But a day's delay would give him time to sort out his thoughts about Tally taking money from strangers. To ponder whether Gött had truly given Tally a miracle or if she was justifying a way to keep money that wasn't hers.

"Tomorrow is Sunday," she said, her tone bordering on impatience. The Amish did not run errands on Sundays. "Besides, what if someone else buys him before then?"

"Maybe someone already has."

Her eyes widened as if that thought had never occurred to her. Or maybe she was stunned by how exasperated he'd sounded. A look of shock fell over her expressive features and, for perhaps the first time in their friendship, the connection between them seemed to have been severed. He could no longer be certain of her thoughts or of her feelings. Had this conflict between them caused a crack in their foundation? The dread he felt inside was more chilling than the winter wind on his skin. He wanted to take his words back, but it was too late.

Tally straightened her shoulders and faked a smile. "I should go. Before I see Mr. Wray, I need to cash the checks. The bank closes at noon."

"You can't go out there alone. Your grandparents would never permit it."

"They've gone to Lancaster for the day."

That was surprising news, especially since Tally hadn't gone with them. A trip to the county seat, which offered a greater variety of stores than those found in Birdsong Falls, was usually a family event. Though the answer was none of his business, he couldn't resist asking the question.

"Why did they go there?"

A shadow crossed Tally's face. "They didn't tell me." She began to walk toward the barn door. Caleb hurried after her, catching up to her before she reached it. He stepped in front of her, forcing her to stop.

"That doesn't make any sense," he said. "They actually went to Lancaster without giving you a reason?"

"Maybe it's a surprise." The hurt in her tone told him she didn't believe their trip was for a pleasant purpose. Then again, maybe the hurt was because they'd left her behind. Or perhaps he had been the one to cause it.

"Please don't go, Tally. Not like this."

"Let me pass, Caleb. If I don't go now, it'll be near dark before I get back home."

"I'll take you." The words popped out of his mouth even before he'd made the conscious decision to go with her. But what choice did he have? He'd be sick with worry if she went without him. "Give me a few minutes to hitch Buttermilk."

"What about Sprout? I can't leave him here."

"We'll drop him off at your farm. It's not that far out of the way."

"I'll go ahead, then. By the time you get there, I'll have him unharnessed and I'll be ready to go."

Caleb nodded his agreement, though he didn't want Tally out of his sight for even a minute. As he helped her into the buggy, he couldn't help feeling that there were undercurrents to this entire situation that he didn't comprehend.

On his way back to the barn to harness Buttermilk, a multitude of questions assaulted him. Why had the Bylers gone to Lancaster without Tally? If she hadn't wanted to go, wouldn't she have told him that? Or had she insisted to them, as she had to him, that this trip to purchase the puppy must be made today? If so, he was dumbfounded that Tally's grandfather hadn't volunteered to take her. Surely the trip to Lancaster could have been postponed until Monday.

Perhaps the Bylers didn't realize how disreputable Mr. Wray had appeared or how rude he'd been. Had Tally told her grandparents about the rumors surrounding the kennel owner? Caleb couldn't believe they'd have allowed Tally to return to the kennels by herself if she had. Though maybe they had believed, even trusted, that Caleb planned to go with her. It was a safe assumption, considering he'd been the one to take her to return the puppy.

Obviously, Caleb should have asked Tally more questions. He turned around, but she and Sprout were already more than halfway down the long lane. It was too late for questions now. All he could do was see her safely to the kennels and back home again.

And pray that, after today, they'd never have a reason to visit Oscar Wray again.

CHAPTER ELEVEN

Caleb helped Tally from the buggy and waited outside while she went inside the bank. They hadn't talked much on the drive from the Byler farm into town. Tally seemed filled with nervous energy, and she'd gripped her drawstring bag as if her life depended on its contents. When he'd mustered the gumption to ask if she truly believed the puppy was worth such a huge amount of money, she'd only smiled—as if that was answer enough. Perhaps it was, since that smile had wrapped around his heart and awakened in him a sudden desire to kiss her.

This wasn't the first time that desire had come over him. It seemed to happen at the oddest—and most inappropriate—times. Like last fall, when several of their neighbors had gathered at the old Keller homestead to help replace his roof. Tally had brought him a glass of water and stood beside him while he drained it. When he handed her the empty glass, their fingers touched, and a current as powerful as a lightning bolt passed between them. They'd held each other's gaze a moment too long, and then, of their own accord, his eyes had flicked to her mouth. He'd immediately turned away, only to see his oldest brother, Jonah, staring at him with a bemused expression on his face. Thankfully, Jonah had never teased him about the awkward moment. If he had, Caleb might have been tempted to snap his brother's suspenders.

One thing he could say with certainty was that their first kiss would not take place in front of family. Nor would he let it happen when he was sweaty from hard labor. And especially not during a buggy ride into town, on an errand that made his insides crawl with doubt and worry.

As he sat perched on the buggy seat, Caleb surveyed the street and tried to still his restless thoughts. As was common for a Saturday in December, quite a few people wandered in and out of the nearby shops, though not nearly as many as would swell the sidewalks during tourist season. Like many other Amish in their district, Caleb tended to make as few trips to town as possible during the summer weekends, when the crowds were at their peak. During those times, he felt more like a zoo exhibit than a longtime member of the community quietly going about his business.

As he exchanged greetings with passing acquaintances, he continued to ponder whether there was any way to postpone the trip to the Wray farm. He couldn't come up with any ideas short of locking Tally in her house. Even if he dared to do something that drastic, what good would it do? She'd be furious with him— and with good reason.

While Caleb believed the scriptural teaching about the husband being the head of his household, he didn't believe that role gave a man the right to squelch his wife's spirit. Those few men he knew who ruled their homes with iron hands, both among the Amish and the Englisch, didn't seem to have happy families. Their example was not one he planned to follow. Instead, he hoped to emulate the respectful partnership of his own parents. They understood that their traditional roles benefited the entire family, but they also supported each other's interests.

Caleb smiled as a well-known proverb flitted through his mind: "The man who claims to be the boss in his own home will lie about other things as well."

How much truth was there in that old saying?

As Caleb continued to look around, his gaze settled on a man with collar-length dark hair who was leaning against a phone booth across the street. The man, who was dressed in jeans and a fleece-lined jacket over a denim shirt, immediately shifted his position so that he no longer faced the buggy. His focused attention on the hardware store's Christmas window display raised the hackles on Caleb's neck. He had the distinct impression the man, who looked to be in his mid- to late forties, had been staring at him.

If Caleb had a dime for all the stares he'd received from strangers during his lifetime, he could have bought Tally a dozen Aussiedoodles. But there was something furtive about this Englischer, as if his interest in Caleb was rooted not in rude curiosity but in something deeper. Perhaps even something more personal.

Caleb shifted his gaze to the bank as Tally emerged through the heavy door. A huge smile lit up her face, and he feigned a smile of his own as he hopped from the buggy to greet her.

"I was able to cash all the checks," she said, her voice brimming with excitement. "Even the out-of-state ones. The bank manager said he trusts me."

"Of course, he does." Caleb had no doubt that Aaron Byler had a nice-sized sum in his personal savings account. Definitely enough to cover any checks that might bounce. He still found it hard to believe her grandfather had approved of her spending so much money for a pet. Neither of Tally's grandparents was known for being overly indulgent with their only grandchild. "Are you certain this is how you want to spend the money?"

Tally looked at him as if she couldn't believe he'd asked her such a question. "What choice do I have? These people gave me the money to care for Scamp. I can't care for him if I don't have him."

Her logic made sense, and yet there was something illogical about this entire situation. Caleb just wasn't sure how to put his misgivings into words. At least not into words that wouldn't make Tally angry with him.

"Then let's go get him." His tone was more subdued than the words themselves, but Tally didn't seem to notice. He started toward the buggy but stopped when Tally didn't follow. Her boots seemed planted in front of the newspaper office.

"I wish we had enough money to buy every dog he has so he'd go out of business," she said.

"With that much money, he'd only get more dogs," Caleb said lightly. The long drive would be miserable if they were both on edge. "At least you'll be giving one special puppy a good home."

Tally grabbed Caleb's hand. "I knew you understood. Danki for being my friend."

Even through her gloves, the spark of her touch caused Caleb's pulse to quicken. Again, he thought to kiss her but held himself back. Not only was this not the time or the place, but her words had also bruised his heart. Somehow he managed to keep the hurt from his voice. "I've always considered us to be more than friends, Tally."

An adorable blush colored her cheeks as her gaze held his. When she spoke, her voice was soft but certain. "I know we are, Caleb. And I'm glad of it."

He straightened her coat collar though it didn't need straightening, then led her to the buggy. As he helped her climb up to the bench seat, he noticed the dark-haired Englischer take a couple of steps in their direction, as if he were about to jaywalk across the street. But when his gaze met Caleb's hard stare, he hesitated, tilted his head down, and turned back to the sidewalk.

Strange behavior by a strange man.

Who was he, and what was he doing here? And why was he so interested in Caleb? Or was his interest in Tally?

As Caleb drove Buttermilk past the hardware store, he glared at the stranger. The man didn't turn away, but he appeared to visibly relax his posture and soften his expression, as if trying to send the message that he wasn't a threat.

Still, Caleb intended to keep an eye out for the man.

He also needed to find a way to convince Tally—without alarming her—not to come into town alone.

CHAPTER TWELVE

Tally's heart lodged in her throat as Buttermilk pulled Caleb's buggy along the drive to Mr. Wray's house. As before, the two watchdogs barked as they approached, alerting anyone within hearing distance of their presence. A moment later, Oscar Wray emerged from the long structure marked with the kennel sign. He held a towel-wrapped bundle in the crook of his arm and went to stand beside a wagon wheel with broken spokes, which stood upright in the dirt.

"Whoa, gal." Caleb gave a slight tug on the reins when they reached the wagon wheel.

"What are the two of you folks doing back here again?" Wray's rough tone seemed more like a challenge than a welcome. But his unfriendliness only strengthened Tally's resolve not to leave without Scamp.

"We came back for the puppy," Caleb said, his tone just as cold. Tally laid a hand on his arm and forced warmth into the smile she directed at Mr. Wray.

"You asked for eight hundred dollars." She held up her drawstring bag. "I have that much money now."

Mr. Wray stared at her, his expression seeming to waver between curiosity and surprise and something else she couldn't define. Cunning, perhaps?

He shifted the bundle in his arm, and a corner of the towel fell open, exposing the rounded muzzle of a tiny puppy. Tally gasped, and Mr. Wray tenderly covered the puppy again. "His momma's not doing too well." All the gruffness had disappeared from his voice. "I've been sittin' with her while waiting for the doc to get here. Sure is takin' his sweet time."

"Is there anything we can do to help?" Tally asked.

Mr. Wray gave her a long, appraising look. Usually such a stare would have made her uncomfortable enough to turn away. But not this time. She sensed his motive wasn't rude curiosity but an attempt to discern the motivation behind her offer.

"I mean that in all sincerity," she said. "If there's anything we can do . . ."

"Nah," he said. "I've been doing this long enough to know a bit about what to do and what not to do when pups are born. Once in a rare while, the doc comes in handy. This is one of those times."

"Then I'll pray he arrives soon." Tally smiled at him, genuinely touched by his concern for the newborn puppy's mother. She'd judged Mr. Wray on gossip and a poor first impression. Now she was seeing him in a different light and regretted her earlier conclusion.

He looked at her a moment more, and Tally got the distinct notion that he was adjusting his view of her too.

"I don't usually let folks go traipsing through the kennels," he finally said. "It's not that I've got anything to hide. Only there's bacteria on shoes that can be dangerous to my littlest ones."

He paused, shifting his gaze to the kennel door and back again. "But you can come into the front office for a moment or two. Get warmed up and we can talk a bit of business." Without waiting for a reply, he returned to the building.

Tally started to climb down from the buggy when Caleb grabbed her arm. "You can't go in there."

"He invited us."

"Because you're being too friendly with him." Caleb released a heavy sigh. "You heard what Bill Edmond said when we were at the newspaper offices. This Englischer doesn't have a good reputation. We should leave."

Tally gently removed Caleb's hand from her arm and squeezed his fingers. "I'm not leaving without Scamp. Besides, I'm beginning to think Mr. Wray is surly because he's lonely."

"Lonely?" Caleb stared at her in disbelief and shook his head. "Is it any wonder? Think about the welcome we got from him only a couple of days ago. That was more than being surly."

"We probably didn't make a very good impression either. But he's giving us a second chance, and we need to give him one too."

"A second chance." Caleb huffed. "I'm not sure that's wise."

"I'm going into his office," Tally said firmly. "I'd appreciate it if you come with me, but you can stay in the buggy if you want."

"You know I can't do that."

"I know." Tally kept her tone light and teasing, hoping it would ease his worry. Besides, what else could she say? Later, she'd have to admit that her grandparents didn't know about this visit and tell him how much she appreciated him leaving his work to come with her. But she couldn't say any of that yet.

Caleb climbed from the buggy and then lifted Tally from the seat. The wary look in his eyes unsettled her, but not enough to dissuade her from accepting Mr. Wray's invitation. Her determination to rescue Scamp from this place had become an obsession. But she was no longer as convinced as she'd been ten minutes before that Scamp actually needed to be rescued.

When they entered the building, Tally drew in a sharp breath. Unsurprisingly, a doggy odor permeated the air. More unexpected was the sharp antiseptic tang of disinfectant that offset it. The long room was divided by a half wall into two uneven sections. The shorter section in which they stood, no more than seven or eight feet deep, appeared to serve as a kind of office, with a desk, shelves, and cabinets. An older-model computer sat on the desk alongside what appeared to be a ledger, various file folders, and stacks of papers.

Tally turned and saw that the bundled-up puppy Mr. Wray had been carrying now lay in a basket under an oblong heating lamp on a table beside the desk. The towel had been pulled back to reveal the puppy's tiny face and ears. A small bottle half-filled with a bluish solution lay next to the bundle. A black-and-tan Yorkie terrier—the pup's mother, Tally assumed—rested in a second basket beneath the same light.

The longer section of the room was filled with cages of varying heights, arranged on one side of an aisle. The cages had obviously seen better days, but they appeared clean. Each one that held a dog also contained a bed, food and water dishes, and a toy or two.

On the other side of the aisle were three fenced areas, each one with an assortment of jumps made from PVC pipe, raised steps to climb on, round chutes, and other toys. Three gangly puppies bounded in the middle section, seemingly oblivious to Tally and Caleb.

Mr. Wray opened one of the cages and knelt down. He spoke in a soft voice, and a moment later, Scamp crawled into his arms. Mr. Wray brought him to Tally. "This the little guy you want? He was busy taking a nap after his playtime."

Scamp yipped and practically launched himself into Tally's arms. "Yes," she said between puppy kisses and examining him from head to tail. His coat was as clean and shiny as when she'd returned him a couple of days ago. "He's put on weight. And I think his legs are longer."

"They change fast at this age." Mr. Wray opened the half door between the two sections of the room and walked around his desk to take a seat. "He does seem to have taken a shine to you."

"This is a nice setup you have here." Caleb tried but failed to hide his surprise. Tally couldn't fault him. She was surprised too.

"Not what you were expecting, is it?"

"Frankly, no," Caleb admitted.

Mr. Wray shifted in his seat and gingerly patted the exhausted Yorkie whose tiny groans indicated she had endured a difficult labor. He then retrieved the newborn puppy and the bottle from the basket. "I've always been one to keep mostly to myself. Prefer it that way." He held the bottle as the puppy noisily sucked on the nipple. "I can't help what others say, even when they're wrong. I'd think you'd know something about that. About being different."

"You're right," Caleb agreed. For the first time since their arrival, his lips were curved into a friendly smile. "We do know something about that."

"If you'd all like a soft drink or a bottle of water, you could probably find one in that little fridge over there." Mr. Wray pointed to a compact refrigerator tucked against the wall opposite the desk.

"No, danki," Tally replied. She took a deep breath and prayed Mr. Wray wouldn't be offended by the question she needed to ask. "Do you mind telling me how this little guy ended up in town trying to cross a busy street?"

"I guess I can, as long as you don't hold it against me."

"I'll do my best not to," Tally said. "But I'd like to know the answer before I make any promises."

"I can respect that." Mr. Wray adjusted his hold on the puppy and the bottle. "He was in the play yard around back when somebody came by asking if he could buy this place. Can you believe that? Why would anyone want my property in the state it's in? It serves me just fine, but no one else needs to be interested. Anyway, by the time I got rid of that nosy trespasser, that there fella was nowhere to be seen." He pointed at Scamp. "I got the rest of the litter back inside and went out looking for him. Trekked across the fields and down the road with no luck at all. I figured never to see him again. But when I went to the newspaper website to place a lost-and-found ad, there he was right at the top of their page. Couldn't hardly believe it."

As Mr. Wray talked, Tally's heart was in a whirl. Scamp rested in her arms as if he belonged there, and she felt a connection with him that she couldn't explain. Another person might argue that she only felt that way because she'd saved him from being injured or killed. But Tally felt the connection ran deeper than that. She'd never had a pet of her own, except for Sprout.

But if she took Scamp home with her, she'd have the same problem she had before. Her grandparents didn't want her to have a dog, so she wouldn't be able to keep him. And yet if she left him behind again, another piece of her heart would shatter.

"Are you still willing to sell him to me?" she asked.

"I stick to my word."

She hugged Scamp close. She didn't want to ask her next question. But she had little choice. The conditions here weren't what she'd been led to believe. The dogs weren't being mistreated or neglected. Instead, all the ones she could see appeared content and healthy.

"What will happen to him if I don't take him?"

Beside her, Caleb stiffened. She refused to look at him, though she knew her question must have been a shock to him after her insistence they make this trip.

Mr. Wray squinted as he once again gave Tally an appraising look. Just as before, she didn't react but simply waited for him to respond.

"I've already had a few inquiries. Won't be no trouble finding him a home."

His answer should have made her happy, but instead, her heart sank. What had she expected him to say? That Scamp would live at the kennel forever? That wasn't something she wanted either.

"I don't sell my little 'uns to just anyone who can write a check, if that's what's botherin' you. I talk to 'em. Find out a bit about 'em. He'll be all right."

Scamp wriggled in Tally's arms, and she realized she had unconsciously tightened her hold. She buried her chin in the pup's soft fur to make it up to him. "You can't know that for sure, though. Can you?"

"People aren't always what they seem, that's sure enough true."

Though his tone stayed even, Tally sensed that he was speaking about himself—and perhaps about them—as much as he was about his potential customers. Around here, people thought of Oscar Wray as something he wasn't. They had been quick to complain about neglect without any proof. Even after the investigations cleared him, his innocence hadn't been believed. Was it because his house was in need of repair and a new coat of paint? Because weeds grew in his junk-littered yard? Because he intimidated people with his quiet demeanor, odd mannerisms, and hermit-like ways?

Tally had made assumptions about him that she'd learned today were wrong and unfair. And for that she was sorry.

But now she had a decision to make. If she didn't take Scamp with her, she'd never see him again. The pain that caused her made no sense, but it was very real. If she did buy him, though, what would she do with him? She couldn't take him home. But perhaps she could find him a home with someone close by so that she could see him often. That way, she'd always know that he was safe and warm and well fed.

That plan seemed fraught with heartache too. But she'd already trusted Gött with one miracle, and He'd come through. Against all odds, people who didn't even know her had sent her more money than she needed. She would now trust Him to show her the path she needed to take next. And to send her another miracle, if one was needed.

When her grandparents found out what she'd done, one would *definitely* be needed.

Before she could let her head overrule her heart, Tally thrust the puppy into Caleb's arms and opened her drawstring bag. "I have cash." She counted out the bills onto the desk. "Eight hundred dollars."

Mr. Wray placed the stack of money in a drawer, asked Tally for her name, and wrote out a receipt. "I give new owners a puppy pack. You can grab one out of that cabinet over there." He pointed toward a metal cabinet on the opposite wall. "There's a small bag of dog food. Information on canine development. A few other odds and ends."

Tally opened the cabinet doors and pulled out one of several canvas bags. She then placed the receipt and the puppy's shot records, which Mr. Wray had pulled from a filing cabinet, inside it. "Danki, Mr. Wray. I promise I'll take good care of him."

"I know you will," he said. The puppy he was holding had fallen asleep with the bottle's nipple still in his mouth. Mr. Wray set down the bottle and placed the puppy, still wrapped in the towel, on his shoulder as if to burp him. "You don't need me to walk you out, do you?"

Tally shook her head, unable to feel offended at the sudden dismissal. She had what she'd come for, and she only wanted to exult in the moment. By the time she got home, maybe she'd have a plan on what to do next. But for now, all she wanted to do was hold Scamp.

Her very own puppy.

At least for today.

Tally breathed a sigh of relief when she realized her grandparents weren't home yet. If they had been, she'd have had to immediately confess to them what she'd done. And confess to Caleb that she hadn't been totally honest with him either. Guilt washed over her, but the warmth of the puppy in her lap made her feel as though the deception had been worthwhile. True, her errand had turned out not to be as noble as she first thought. She'd imagined herself saving the puppy from horrible conditions. Perhaps somehow even saving all of Mr. Wray's dogs from a puppy mill life.

But then she'd seen Mr. Wray's kennels and learned there was no puppy mill. Only a lonely man who related to dogs better than he did to people. Who cared more for their surroundings than he cared about his own.

Thankfully, Caleb didn't linger. He hadn't said much on the way home, and Tally had the distinct impression he felt troubled by their encounter with Mr. Wray. But surely, Caleb had seen what Tally had seen—that this puppy belonged to her. She wasn't saving Scamp from anything now, but she had saved him once before. Surely that still counted for something.

Caleb might not understand Tally's decision, but she hoped he respected it.

Though perhaps expecting his respect was asking too much, considering that she'd been less than honest with him. She'd explain everything to him someday soon. But first she had to figure out what to tell her grandparents.

Before Caleb left, he asked if she would be spending the rest of the day at home. She'd told him yes. Although she'd told her grandparents she'd return the packages to the post office today, she hadn't had time to rewrap them or to put on new address labels. She also wanted to write a note to include with each returned gift.

As Caleb drove away, Tally took Scamp to the barn so she could check on the horses and other livestock. She made him a bed in an empty stall where he could stay while she did her chores. As she poured dog food into a bowl, she wished again that Nicole could have taken Scamp. Her stomach clenched.

Caleb's poems.

She'd been so preoccupied with Scamp, she'd completely forgotten that she was supposed to pick up Caleb's book of poetry from Nicole today. She couldn't leave Scamp in the stall in case her grandparents returned home before she did. Grossdaddi always checked on the animals when he'd been gone from home any length of time. But she couldn't take Scamp with her either. Mr. Collins was often at the Bouquet Bliss on Saturdays.

Moving quickly, Tally transferred Scamp, his bedding, and the bowls of food and water to a deep box in the woodshed. He'd be safe and warm there until her return. Next, she hurried to the kitchen and left a note saying she was with Nicole. Then she hitched Sprout to the buggy and was on her way. The tote-box with the packages was still in the buggy—she'd put it there before going to the Schwartz farm and hadn't taken it out when she'd returned earlier with Sprout. Just as well. Maybe Nicole could help her with the repackaging.

When Tally drove by the general store on her way to the florist shop, she noticed an Englischer walking toward her along the sidewalk. Usually she wouldn't have given him a second look, but she'd noticed the same man earlier in the day when she came out of the bank. She'd gotten the sense then that he'd been watching her, although the notion had seemed silly at the time. Now, he caught her gaze and then immediately turned away, as if he were embarrassed. As he should be. Rude tourist.

Yet something in the way he looked at her, and in the way he'd turned away, didn't strike her as the typical actions of a tourist. The man had looked at her as if he knew her, but she was certain she'd never seen him before in her life. Still, in the moment after she passed him, something caused her to look back through the buggy's plastic window. He'd stopped and was watching her. A tremble went up her spine, and Tally was thankful when Sprout turned into the alleyway beside the florist shop. She wasn't afraid, exactly, but she planned to be watchful all the same.

Tally decided not to tell Nicole about the stranger. There wasn't anything to tell, anyway, and it wouldn't take many details for Nicole's imagination to take off like one of those rockets at Cape Canaveral in Florida. Tally had seen two or three televised launches at Nicole's house through the years.

When she carried the tote-box into the break room, she found Nicole arranging a bouquet of red and white roses. "I'd about given up on you," Nicole said. "What have you been up to today?"

"You'll never guess. But first, I have to see the book. Did it come?"

"It's over there on the counter."

Tally found the padded envelope and removed the leather-bound book. The title, which Tally had chosen from one of her favorite poems, and Caleb's name were printed on the front in a bold and impressive script. "I can't believe I'm holding this. It's beautiful." Tally opened the book to the title page. It read:

When Sunlight Falls
A Collection of Original Poems
By
Caleb Jonathan Schwartz

"Do you think Caleb will be pleased?" Tally asked as she carefully turned the pages.

"I know he will be." Nicole pursed her lips. She looked as if she was about to explode with some news. "There's something I need to tell you." She wiped her hands on her apron, then retrieved a sheet of paper from the shop's printer. "I know I should have asked you first, but I was afraid you'd say no. And you know that old saying, 'Sometimes it's better to ask for forgiveness than permission.'"

Tally had heard Nicole use that saying before, and she'd never quite accepted it as true. But today, her stomach knotted when she heard the words. That's exactly what she was doing with Scamp. Planning to ask her grandparents for their forgiveness since she hadn't asked for their permission. Though that wasn't quite accurate. She *had* asked for permission and been told no. Did that mean they would also refuse their forgiveness?

A week or so ago, she wouldn't have been able to imagine such a thing. But over the past few days, they'd been acting so strange that now anything seemed possible. Their anger at her outright disobedience might be more than any of them could handle. And what would happen then?

"Are you listening to me?" Nicole's voice, now shrill, broke into Tally's thoughts.

"Sorry." Tally smiled at her friend. "What did you do that needs forgiveness?"

"This." Nicole handed her the printout of an email from Indiana University.

"Is this where you're planning to go after you graduate from community college? I thought you wanted to go to Penn State."

"It's not from the admissions office." Nicole pointed at the message. "Don't you see? It's a university press, like a small publisher that specializes in books that the big publishers don't want. They're interested in Caleb's poems."

"Caleb's poems? But how would they know—"

"I sent them a copy of his manuscript. Isn't it exciting?" Nicole practically squealed. "I didn't send it only to them, mind you, but they were the first to respond. And they want to publish it. Don't you see, Tally? Caleb's poems won't only be in one single book you give him for a Christmas present. His poems will be in a book and sold online and in the university bookstore and who knows where else. He might even be famous someday."

Nicole's words drew Tally out of her misery over her grandparents and made her consider Caleb. "I doubt Caleb wants to be famous."

"Okay, maybe not famous. But everyone wants to be remembered, to leave a legacy. Besides, this is a tremendous opportunity for him. They don't give contracts to just anybody. He's very talented, and that talent should be appreciated by more than his family and friends."

"Ja, he has a gift." Yet Tally had always considered that gift a personal one, not something to be shared with the outside world. His poems had been intended for her and his family. Now Nicole wanted to show strangers these insights into Caleb's heart and soul. Maybe she never should have let Nicole read any of the poems.

"I'm sorry to say this, Tally, but it isn't your decision. It's Caleb's." The disappointment Nicole obviously felt at her reaction dripped from every word. "I thought you'd want to be the one to tell him. That you'd be excited for him. But if not, then I'll give him the message. They need an answer in a few days."

Nicole's quiet condemnation brought Tally up short. "You're right. It is his decision, and I'm sure he'll be grateful. He would never have thought to send his writings to a place like this."

"That's why you have me as your nearest and dearest friend." Nicole's tone was cheerful again, even teasing. "Because I'm 'Englisch' and think of things that you, smart as you are, do not."

"That you do." Tally tucked the printed email inside the padded envelope alongside Caleb's leather-bound book. "I'll give the message to Caleb when I see him." But she already knew what his answer would be. Caleb didn't care about legacies or being remembered. He cared about his farm and his family and his community. He cared about his future . . . hopefully one that included her.

But for that to happen, he would need to forgive her for her lack of honesty. She shoved the distressing thought away. When the time came, she would explain and Caleb would understand. They'd laugh about all of this in the future. In the present, though, she still had a dilemma. What was she going to do about Scamp?

Mrs. Collins poked her head in the doorway and gave her daughter the orders for three arrangements. While Nicole finished the bouquet of roses and completed the new orders, Tally wrote thank-you notes and prepared the packages she needed to return. As they worked, Tally told her friend about the visit to Mr. Wray's kennel and her purchase of Scamp. Nicole was so sure that her grandparents would let her keep the puppy that Tally half believed they would too. Once the last package was ready to mail, she loaded all her items and Caleb's precious book into the totebox. The post office had closed at noon, but the local pack-and-ship store stayed open late on Saturdays.

By the time Tally arrived home, she was physically and emotionally exhausted. Her grandparents still weren't home, and Tally's mood swung between feeling gratitude for the extra time with Scamp and irritation that they'd stayed away so long.

She took Scamp to the barn and played with him there until a motor sounded in the driveway. Then she quickly returned him to the woodshed and raced into the house. By now, her irritation had hardened into obstinacy. At first she'd worried about how to tell her grandparents about Scamp. Now she wondered how long she could hide him until they found him.

After all, if they weren't going to tell her their secret, why should she tell them hers?

CHAPTER THIRTEEN

Caleb accepted the cup of coffee and slice of apple cinnamon strudel that Iris Byler set before him. Sunday services were held every other week in their district. The off-weeks were for visiting family and friends. Though he and Tally hadn't made plans to spend the day together, he had decided to come anyway. He wanted to see if Scamp had kept her up all night. At least that was his excuse. Mostly, he wanted to apologize for his recent moodiness and to try to repair any cracks that might be starting to form in their foundation.

Truth be told, he wanted to give her an opportunity to apologize too. Her behavior had also been odd. During the entire trip the previous day, first to the bank and then to Oscar Wray's kennel, the two of them had been out of sync with each other.

"Eat up," Iris urged him. "Tally should be back any moment. I don't know why it takes her so long to gather a few eggs."

"She gets to dreaming, she does," Aaron said. "Always has been one to let her mind go wandering."

"Such shenanigans are for Kinna," Iris retorted, "not a girl who'll be twenty soon."

Caleb hid a smile. He'd heard comments like these from Tally's grandparents before. He understood that Iris wanted Tally to be more practical, but Caleb appreciated her dreaming ways. At least most of the time. Yesterday he'd felt frustrated by how lost in her own world she'd been on the drive to the Wray farm. And by her secretiveness.

"She's probably busy teaching Scamp not to chase the hens," he said, hoping to lighten the moment.

Aaron stared at him, his fork halfway between his plate and his mouth, while Iris let out an audible gasp. Caleb looked from one to the other, his stomach sinking. What had he said?

"That dog isn't here," Iris exclaimed. She glared at her husband. "Is he?"

"Not that I know of." Aaron rested his fork on his plate. "You were there when she returned him to that man. Wray. Wasn't that his name?"

"We did take him back." Caleb felt like he was dragging his words from the mud, pulling each one free only with great effort. "But we went back for him yesterday. She must have told you." How could she not have told them?

Nobody said a word. Anger and disappointment rose within Caleb, rendering the sweet strudel in his mouth tasteless. Not only hadn't Tally told her grandparents about her plans, but she'd also led him to believe they had given her permission to buy the puppy. Hadn't she?

His mind went over the conversations they'd had yesterday. He couldn't pinpoint a specific lie she'd told him. And yet she had not been honest.

"I should go." He scooted his chair backward. "If I'd known . . ." What? He wouldn't have taken her to the kennel? But she'd been so determined to go, there was no way—permission or not— that he would have let her go alone. And yet her guilt was now his guilt too. He didn't like it. But he was man enough to accept it. "I am sorry."

"Before you go," Aaron said, "I have one question I'd like you to answer."

Caleb nodded and prayed it would be a question he could answer honestly without causing Tally more trouble with her grandparents.

"Did you buy the puppy for her?"

Caleb hesitated, his mind whirling to make sense of the undercurrents beneath the question. Across the table from him, Iris fumed. Her lips were pressed into a tight line, and the wrinkles around her mouth were deeply etched.

"Give me the respect of an honest answer." Aaron's voice was low, barely above a whisper.

"I wouldn't do anything less." Caleb took a deep breath, his frustration at Tally growing in the wake of the rift she'd caused between him and her grandfather. He chose his words carefully. "Tally had her own money."

Iris pushed her chair back so quickly it almost fell over. She steadied it, nearly stumbling as she did so, then left the room. Her husband's gaze followed her, and then he sighed and slowly rose. "Danki, Caleb."

The back door flew open, and Tally hurried into the kitchen still wearing her snow-covered boots.

"Caleb," she said too brightly. "I didn't expect you this morning."

"There you are," Aaron said before Caleb could respond. "Your grandmother and I were thinking about forming a search party."

"I was doing my chores."

"What about Scamp?" Aaron asked. "Where's he?"

Tally shifted her glance from Caleb to her grandfather and back again. Caleb held her gaze, hoping she could see both his disappointment and his regret for having spilled her secret. More than anything, he wished he'd gone to visit Daniel this morning instead. Or that he'd gone to the old Keller homestead. He wouldn't work on the Sabbath, but he'd have enjoyed the quiet there, the peace. And he would have dreamed the dreams that might now be ruined.

Tally lowered her eyes, and her shoulders bowed. "He's in the woodshed."

"I guess he can stay there for a spell. Though this is a sorry mess you've made." Without another word, Aaron left the room.

Caleb waited for Tally to raise her eyes. When she did, her unshed tears caused his heart to fall into his stomach. He wanted to go to her. He wanted to escape the house. But his feet seemed rooted to the floor. He didn't know what to do or what to say. Though he ached for an explanation, he didn't want to make any accusations. Especially not when his own thoughts were so muddled.

Was he angry because she'd pulled him into her deception and risked his relationship with her grandparents? Or was he hurt because she hadn't trusted him enough to be honest with him?

He knew the answer. It was both these things.

Something his brother once said flitted through Caleb's mind. When Daniel was courting Deborah, they'd once had a minor disagreement that spiraled into hurt feelings and a deeper misunderstanding. "When you don't know what to say, sometimes it's best to say nothing," Daniel had told Caleb. Daniel had regretted not following his own advice at the time. Caleb decided to heed his brother's words now.

"I should go," he said. "You'll want to talk with your grandparents."

Tally looked miserable, but she didn't say anything. Caleb slipped past her and out the back door. He was almost to his buggy when the door opened behind him.

"Wait a minute," Tally called. "Caleb, please wait."

He moved to Buttermilk's head and checked her bridle while he waited. When Tally reached the buggy, she held out a package wrapped in brown paper and tied with a silver ribbon. "I know it's early, but I want you to have this. *Freulich Kristag.*" Merry Christmas.

"Christmas is still a couple of weeks away. Why are you giving this to me now?"

"Why not?" The warmth of her smile failed to reach her eyes. Her expression was uncertain, as if she were no longer sure of his affection for her. As hurt as he'd felt by her actions, this realization hurt him even more. Had his trust in her been so shaken that his feelings for her were no longer as clear and steadfast as he'd believed? If so, what did that say about him? About his constancy? His faithfulness?

"Please open it," she urged.

He walked with her toward the side of the buggy, which helped shelter them from the wind, and untied the ribbon. When he opened the box and saw what was inside, all words escaped him. The leather-bound book had his name on the cover, something he'd never imagined he'd see.

"This is beautiful." He ran his fingers along the engraved text and opened the book to a random page. The poem, one he'd written, had no title. Few of his poems did. But he remembered the day he'd written it. He'd found an arrowhead in the field, which inspired thoughts of a long-ago century during which another man had walked this land. That man's way of life seemed primitive to Caleb's eyes, just as Caleb's way of life seemed primitive to his Englisch neighbor. Yet God created the land to provide food and shelter for each of them, sending both sunshine and rain for their harvests.

Overcome with emotion, Caleb gently closed the book and ran his hand over his eyes.

"You don't like it?" Tally's voice sounded small, almost childlike. "How . . ." He paused to clear his throat. "How did you do this?" "Eliza and I gathered your poems together." He could hear both hope and uncertainty in Tally's tone. "Nicole found a printer in Philadelphia who made it and bound it." "It's a beautiful gift, Tally. One I'll always cherish. Danki." When she didn't answer, Caleb met her gaze. Her eyes still glistened, but her voice was steady. "I have something to tell you." Caleb's shoulders tensed. Was this it? Had their foundation become irreparably cracked before they'd even had a chance to begin their home together? He braced himself and waited for the hammer to drop on his heart.

"I'm not sure what you'll think of this," Tally said, "but Nicole sent your poems to a small university press in Indiana. They want to publish the manuscript." She pulled a folded piece of paper from her coat pocket. "This is the email they sent her with the contract details. They even want to pay you an advance."

The words Tally spoke were so different than what Caleb had been expecting that it took him a moment to process them. Even then, they didn't make any sense to him. He took the email from her and skimmed the words of the message.

This was unbelievable. He hadn't written his poems for Nicole or the editor of a university press.

"Look what the editor said." Tally pointed to a sentence in the email. "*Mr. Schwartz shows a remarkable talent for evoking emotion with his precise imagery.*"

The words stunned him, lifting him up with their praise. But could he believe them? "They're only scribblings," he protested.

"The editor doesn't think so." Tally straightened her posture. "Neither do I."

"I thank you for the book, Tally. It means a great deal to me that you'd go to so much trouble." Though even in this moment, his feelings felt mixed. He knew Tally's actions were well intentioned.

She'd put time and thoughtfulness into the gift. He didn't want to seem unappreciative. And yet . . .

"I was glad to do it, Caleb. Now your poems are a legacy you can pass down to your children and your grandchildren. They'll know what a fine man you are. What a good man you are."

Caleb's cheeks warmed under her praise. Though he wasn't sure he deserved her compliments. "It's a kind thought. And a treasured gift."

"What will you do about the contract?"

"I can't tell you right now." His first inclination was to say no, but he didn't want to act in haste. He especially didn't want to rush into a decision that might widen the cracks between them. "It's not a situation I ever imagined."

"Me either. I was stunned when Nicole told me."

"She shouldn't have done it without asking."

"You're right," Tally agreed. "But she meant well."

Caleb reached for Tally's hand and gazed deep into her eyes. "What about you, Tally? Why didn't you tell me your grandparents didn't know what you planned to do yesterday?"

Tally's posture stiffened, but she didn't pull away. "People sent me the money for Scamp. I prayed for a miracle, and God answered my prayer."

He squeezed her fingers. "You should have told me."

"Would you have gone with me if I had?"

"I never would have let you go out there alone."

"I am sorry, Caleb. I couldn't take that chance." She slipped her hand from his and took a step back. "Freulich Kristag, Caleb."

Before he could respond, she raced toward the woodshed. He considered going after her, but what good would that do? What else was there to say now?

"When you don't know what to say, sometimes it's best to say nothing."

CHAPTER FOURTEEN

Now that the secret was out, Tally allowed herself to carry Scamp from the woodshed to the house. Once they were inside the mudroom, she brushed the dirt and wood shavings from his fur. Scamp kept her busy with his attempts to either bite at the brush or escape, and the rhythmic action helped soothe her unruly emotions. She didn't know why she'd chosen that moment to give Caleb his Christmas present. It definitely hadn't been the moment of her dreams.

In her daydreams about giving him the book, they'd always been alone in his buggy on a crisp winter night, delivering Christmas packages of baked goods and canned preserves to their friends and neighbors. In her imagination, once all the deliveries were made, she pulled out one more present. His.

That scenario would never happen now, the opportunity ruined by her impetuousness. But the acquisitions editor at the university press needed an answer in a few days, and Tally couldn't tell Caleb about the email until after she'd given him the book.

Besides, she had needed an excuse to talk to him before he left, and the book had provided that. She'd meant to apologize for her lack of honesty and ask for his forgiveness. But the pain in his eyes had been unbearable. The proof of how she'd hurt him had set her nerves on edge and caused her to feel defensive. These weren't emotions she was used to feeling, at least not to this extent. Her life, until about a week ago, had been wrapped up in a cozy quilt of routine and stability. Sure, a few threads were frayed, such as her occasional envy of Nicole and her hurt feelings concerning her grandparents' reluctance to talk about their past. But those frayed emotions hadn't dominated her life.

Everything had changed the moment she'd run into the street to rescue Scamp. The photographs the strangers had taken of her had ushered the outside world into their tranquil home, bringing pride, fear, anger, and, yes, deceit to their doorstep.

"See how much trouble you've caused." She allowed Scamp to lick her fingers, then turned him around to brush his hind legs. "Your name suits you."

Her emotions and thoughts swung back and forth as fast as Scamp's stubby tail.

If only Caleb had stayed home this morning. Then she could have told her grandparents about the puppy when she was ready to do so. Then she wouldn't have given him his Christmas present out of guilt instead of love.

Though it wasn't fair to blame him. Her own willful nature had also played a part in everything that had happened. She'd been horrified when the first photograph appeared on the paper's website, but she'd been secretly proud of its attractiveness. Of *her* attractiveness. The presents and letters had added to her pride.

Somewhere along the way, she'd gotten the notion that she didn't need to listen to her grandparents but could make her own decisions, even when those decisions affected them. She'd deceived those she loved most to get what she wanted instead of sacrificing what she wanted to keep their trust.

She hugged Scamp to her, wishing she understood why this little ball of fur meant so much to her that she couldn't let him go. Somehow she had to convince her grandparents that, despite her recent actions, she still loved and respected them. She needed to apologize to them—something she'd failed to do with Caleb.

But she couldn't do so yet. She wasn't ready to tell them she'd gotten up early and hidden the Sunday edition of the *Birdsong Banner*. Her photo had appeared on the bottom half of the first page. This time, her name was included in the accompanying article.

It had been a childish thing to do. She knew that. Yet she could only handle one crisis at a time. She decided that she'd give them the paper after they'd talked about Scamp.

Tally carried the puppy into the house and found her grandparents in the living room. The heavy metal doors of the stove were open, and Grossdaddi was adding a log to the fireplace. Grossmammi sat in her rocker, knitting the afghan for the neighbors' Christmas box.

Tally perched on the hearth with Scamp in her lap. Grossmammi rocked harder as she glared at the puppy. "Dogs don't belong inside the house."

"You're right."

"Yet here he is. As if this were a home for stray animals instead of a working farm. He can never earn his keep or repay in any way what you spent on him. I thought we'd taught you the value of a dollar and the importance of honesty."

Grossmammi's words struck Tally's conscience as hard as thrown pebbles. At least until she'd uttered that last phrase.

"Honesty?" True, Tally had been dishonest, but she wasn't the only one who'd kept her own counsel. Still, she'd never been one to question her grandparents, and she found it difficult to do so even now when the desire—no, the need—to defend herself seemed to override all reason.

"You're wondering why we went to Lancaster yesterday." Grossdaddi slowly moved from the fireplace to his recliner. But instead of leaning back and popping up the footrest, he kept the chair upright. "We weren't going to tell you until tomorrow, but circumstances being what they are"—he gestured toward Scamp—"it seems we have no choice except to tell you now." He sighed deeply. "You never should have brought him back here, Talitha. That choice will only cause you more heartache."

"I know I should have told you my plan," Tally said. "I'm sorry I didn't. But Scamp means the world to me. I can't explain why because it doesn't make sense, even to me. I just know that we belong together. Please don't make me give him up. Not again."

The forcefulness of her tone scared her. She wasn't used to talking to her grandparents so boldly. She rarely shared her inmost thoughts and feelings with them. But the inner nudging to stand up for herself somehow gave her the courage to do exactly that.

Scamp settled in her lap as if the brushing had worn him out. His dense fur warmed Tally's fingers as she absentmindedly stroked his back. His very existence had revealed something hidden within her and within her grandparents. They'd become strangers to one another, each with their own secrets.

Maybe their relationship had a fragile veneer all along, and the puppy's rescue had cracked it. Perhaps they weren't the strong, tight-knit family they'd always believed themselves to be. Instead of Tally *and* her grandparents, the dynamic now seemed to be Tally *versus* her grandparents. None of them wanted it to be that way, she was sure. At the same time, none of them seemed to know how to go back to the way they'd been.

"It's not your place to make a decision like that on your own," Grossmammi snapped. She dabbed at her forehead with a handkerchief. "Not while you're living under our roof."

"Now, Iris," Grossdaddi said softly. "There's no need to make this situation more difficult than it already is."

"I'm well aware of the situation, Aaron. Of all people, you should know this isn't easy for me either."

"I know, Iris. Believe me, I know." His eyes clouded over as he stared at the fire. He released a heavy sigh, then shifted his gaze to Tally. His thin lips curved into a tender smile. "Grossmammi and I have a special surprise for you. We're going to Florida for Christmas. We might even visit one of the theme parks we've heard so much about. I think I'd like to go to Epcot. They have attractions about other countries there. We can try the fish and chips from England and take a ride inside that big white ball."

Tally lowered her eyes and focused on stroking Scamp's fur. Perhaps this was the moment to tell them what she'd overheard the other night. Or would her confession only make things worse by adding to their growing list of her wrongdoings?

"Wouldn't you like to leave this cold weather for a while?" Grossdaddi asked.

"Do you mean we won't be here for Christmas Day?" Tally asked. "What about the afghan Grossmammi is knitting for the Christmas box? And all the baking and the caroling? Are we going to miss everything?"

"We already have the tickets," Grossmammi said. "We're leaving tomorrow, so you need to find something to do with that dog today."

Tally stared at her grandmother as a thousand responses raced through her mind. They already had the tickets? For *tomorrow*?

"I can't take him back." She swallowed back tears. "I won't."

"He can't stay here by himself," Grossdaddi said. "And we can't take him with us. You'll have to return him today, even though it's Sunday. There's no other choice. I'm sorry, Tally. I know you're fond of Scamp. But this is the consequence of making a decision in haste and without seeking our counsel."

Tally bit her lip to avoid saying something she'd regret. This was also the consequence of her grandparents keeping secrets from her. Even though she'd overheard them talking about the trip, she never fully believed they'd really plan one. Their secretive trip to Lancaster probably should have warned her of their intentions, but she'd been too caught up in her own secretive trip to give much thought to theirs. She'd only felt thankful they were away from home for the day so they wouldn't question her own absence.

Grossdaddi rose from his chair. "Get your coat, Tally. I'll drive you to this place and explain to Mr. Wray why we can't keep the puppy."

"Be sure he returns your money. All of it." Grossmammi rubbed her arms and grimaced as if they ached. Yesterday's trip had no doubt tired her out. "There's no need to let him cheat you."

The last thing Tally wanted was for her grandfather to go with her as if she were a Kinner unable to make decisions on her own.

"Caleb will take me. He already knows the way."

"So do you," Grossdaddi said. "You can give me the directions as we go."

"I'm not sure I can find it. Since Caleb was driving, I didn't pay close attention. Maybe Eliza and Sadie will want to go along with us."

Grossdaddi walked over to Tally and laid a wrinkled hand on her head. Beneath his bushy brows, compassion shone in his eyes. "Ja. It will be *gut* for you to spend time with your friends when your heart is heavy. I'll go tell Deacon Fisher about our trip. One of his sons should be willing to look after the livestock while we're away."

"Don't stay away too long, either one of you," Grossmammi said. Her rocking had fallen back to a gentle creak, and the rhythmic clack of the knitting needles had also slowed. "We have preparations to make for the trip."

Tally nodded, but her throat was blocked with a lump, and she couldn't speak. Tears wouldn't change her grandparents' hearts, and she didn't want to humiliate herself further by crying in their presence. She rose slowly from the hearth, carried Scamp to the mudroom, and put on her coat.

Though Tally had headed for the Schwartz farm when leaving home, in the end she'd been unable to bring herself to ask Caleb for another favor. Not after the way they'd left things between them. Asking him to drive her back to Mr. Wray's kennel wouldn't mend the rift. She was afraid it might even give him more reason to be upset with her.

Once she got to town, she'd driven to Nicole's house first, but no one was home. She drove Sprout to Birch Street, praying she'd find her friend at the florist shop. Though the business was never open on Sundays, Nicole and her mom sometimes stopped in to work on floral arrangements or tidy up the place. But neither of their cars were parked in the usual places, and the shop was dark. Sprout wanted to turn into the alley, but Tally urged him forward to an open parking space.

Scamp whimpered beside her on the buggy seat, and Tally drew him into her lap. Now what was she going to do? She'd hoped Nicole would have an idea, or perhaps she'd take care of the puppy while Tally was gone, despite her father's allergies. It was a vain hope, and she knew one friend shouldn't ask another for such a favor. But Tally had no other options except to go back to Mr. Wray. How could she do that?

She bowed her head over the puppy as uncontrollable sobs shook her shoulders.

"Excuse me, miss." A masculine voice spoke softly beside her. Tally's head snapped up in surprise. The stranger she'd seen near the bank yesterday stood near the front of the buggy. He was close enough that he didn't have to raise his voice to be heard, but he was still keeping a respectable distance between them. The concerned look in his eyes appeared genuine.

"Are you okay? Is there something I can do? Someone I can call?"

A strange sensation washed over Tally. She was alone on a sparsely crowded street with an Englischer who'd had the nerve to speak to her. She'd been warned often enough about this precise danger that she knew she should feel frightened.

Except she wasn't afraid. Even though she'd felt alarmed yesterday when she saw him watching her, today she only felt that he somehow seemed familiar. As if she should know him.

"My name is Franklin Thayer." He gave a self-conscious shrug and grinned. "Most people call me Tripp. I don't suppose you've ever heard of me."

"No." The syllable came out short and gruff. Tally sniffed and dug a handkerchief from her coat pocket to wipe her eyes.

"I'm not surprised about that." He glanced toward the puppy. "Who's this little fella?"

"That's a long story," Tally said, feeling as if her heart was splintering once again.

"I've got time to hear a long story if you've got the time to tell it." He pointed toward Birdie's Café. "I've enjoyed a few meals in that place over the past couple of days and can highly recommend the blackberry pandowdy. There's something about that sweet berry goodness that chases away the blues. How about I treat you to a helping?"

Tally shifted her gaze from the diner to Tripp and back again while she considered his offer. Was he someone she should be afraid of? Or was he an answer to her prayer?

There was only one way to find out.

CHAPTER FIFTEEN

Caleb went straight from the Byler farm to the old Keller homestead. He saw several buggies outside his parents' house when he and Buttermilk drove past, but he wasn't in the mood to visit with family and neighbors. Not after the morning he'd spent with Tally and her grandparents.

When he got to the homestead, he carried Tally's gift with him into the house. The rooms were cold, so he laid the package on the fireplace mantel and got a fire going. The process took him longer than usual, either because the wood wasn't completely dry or because of his unsettled mood. But eventually, the glowing embers grew into a small flame that licked at the kindling. He carefully fanned the flame with a piece of cardboard until the first wood log caught fire.

Still huddled in his coat, he retrieved Tally's present and then perched on the hearth and stretched out his legs. What a strange and unsettling morning.

He still couldn't believe he'd revealed Tally's secret to her grandparents. Though he blamed himself for the trouble he'd caused, he also blamed Tally. Why hadn't she told him her grandparents didn't know she intended to purchase the puppy?

The answer of course was simple: they had been adamantly opposed to the idea. Yet Tally had gone against their wishes and tricked Caleb into helping her. He had been angry with her, and he supposed he probably still should be, but he could no longer get the anger to stick.

Each time he tried, the memory of Tally taking Scamp from Mr. Wray filled his mind's eye. And his heart. She'd looked so happy. So . . . fulfilled. It was as if Scamp filled an empty place deep within her—a place Caleb hadn't even known existed.

He opened the package and removed the book, then ran his fingers down the rich, textured leather and traced over his name. Somehow this book, filled with words he'd written, filled an empty place deep within *him*. He didn't want to give in to the sin of pride, but was it wrong to be proud of the words he'd written? Was all pride a sin?

When one of Deacon Fisher's prize bulls fetched a good price at the stock auction, the man didn't gloat, but neither did he dismiss the congratulations of his neighbors. When Eliza's strawberry-rhubarb jam won the blue ribbon at the fair last summer, no one had chided her for being prideful, though she had beamed with happiness.

Was his talent for writing poetry a lesser gift than Deacon Fisher's eye for good stock or Eliza's skill in the kitchen? The Creator of the universe had given Caleb the vision to see what others seemed to miss, and he had an ear for rhythm and sound. Most poems took time and effort to create. A few whispered to him as if they were long-forgotten melodies demanding to be remembered and sung once again.

To deny that gift seemed a false humility—a sin akin to immodest pride.

Despite his earlier misgivings, he realized that Tally couldn't have given him a more thoughtful gift. She was right. A collection of poems with his name on the book's cover was a treasure to pass along to his children. The publishing contract was something else to consider. He unfolded the printed email and read it carefully. The advance was modest, less than Tally had paid for Scamp, and the initial print run was for five hundred copies. If he accepted the offer, his poetry would be shared with a literary world he didn't understand and where he'd never feel he belonged.

In all his years, he'd neither wanted fame nor sought it. He doubted a few hundred copies of a poetry book would bring him any recognition and, truth be told, he wouldn't want them to. All he wanted from life was to farm his own land, to rebuild this house into a home, and to wake up each morning with Tally by his side.

Tally.

Without her, none of his other dreams mattered.

He flipped through the pages of the book, stopping to read a poem here and there. Each one had been written either to Tally or to someone in his family. He valued privacy and so was relieved to know that neither Tally nor Eliza had snooped through his personal journals to gather the poems he'd written there. When he reached the end of the book, he found a note stuck between the last page and the back cover. Tally had written it the day before, after their trip to get Scamp.

> *Dearest Caleb,*
> *Since that first day Scamp leaped into my life, he has become as special to me as Sprout. In a way even more so. I can't explain my affection for him to myself, so I don't know how to explain it to you. I don't have your gift for words.*

But I need you to know that I didn't want any-
one to call me a hero or take my picture. That's
been the most unsettling thing out of all this cra-
ziness. There's something inside me that hates the
attention, but another side of me likes it. I suppose
that's the vain side. The truth is, I still wish the pic-
tures hadn't been taken. But since they were, I'm
glad they're pretty.

There! I said it. And I feel guilty for saying such
a thing. For even thinking it.

I try to push all that aside, though, and think
of the blessings. Because of the pictures, I was given
enough money to get Scamp. And so I did. I pray
I get to keep him despite my pride and my deceit.

Tally

Caleb read the note a second time, then clutched it to his chest. In her own way, Tally was going through the same thing he was. They were both stumbling over their pride amid circumstances neither of them had any control over. She had rushed into danger to rescue a helpless creature, that was all. It wasn't her fault that others had taken photos and shared them across social media.

For his part, Caleb hadn't asked Tally for such a personal Christmas gift, nor had he asked Nicole to send his poems to a publisher. But both had taken initiative on his behalf and the offer had been made. The contract was a blessing that had come to him unexpectedly, just as Scamp had arrived as an unexpected blessing for Tally.

The difference was that Tally was fighting for what she wanted, even at the risk of angering her grandparents, while Caleb wasn't sure what he wanted to do.

He recalled the scene in Tally's home before he left. Her grandmother's anger had filled the room with a dense gloom, while her grandfather took on the roles of both agitated peacemaker and benevolent-but-firm head of the household.

Caleb had known the Bylers for as long as he could remember. Aaron and Iris were fine people who cared deeply about their granddaughter. They were stricter than Caleb's own parents, perhaps because they were of an older generation. Yet he couldn't help but sense, in hindsight, that there had been an odd undercurrent in the kitchen that morning. A tension that had everyone in the family wound up. And that was even before he'd asked about the puppy.

He tucked Tally's note into the pages of the book and returned it to its box. He needed to see her, to make amends for not having understood what she was experiencing. For having been angry because she hadn't trusted him.

Though he wouldn't try to talk the Bylers into letting Tally keep Scamp, he could volunteer to keep him for her. As he extinguished the fire and banked the hot ashes, he looked around the large, drafty room. His plan had been to move into the house with Tally after they married. But there was no reason he and Scamp couldn't move in now. His older brothers should be willing to help him do enough repairs to the kitchen and one of the bedrooms for him to be comfortable here on his own.

The plan made sense, but only if Tally said yes to both his proposals. First, he would ask her to let him take Scamp, and then he would ask her to spend her life with him. Or maybe he should reverse the order and ask her to marry him before he volunteered to keep the dog.

Either way, he needed to see her. Now!

CHAPTER SIXTEEN

Tripp Thayer had removed his corduroy jacket and tucked Scamp inside it before ushering Tally into the diner. Thankfully, the puppy seemed content to take a nap beside her on the booth seat. The waitress raised her eyebrow when the jacket moved a bit, then gave a conspiratorial wink and asked what they wanted to drink.

Tripp ordered two servings of blackberry pandowdy with scoops of homemade vanilla ice cream and two mugs of hot chocolate. After the waitress left, he rested his forearms on the table. "I've told you my name, but you haven't told me yours."

"I'm Talitha Byler." She gave a self-conscious shrug, then realized the gesture mimicked the one he'd given her when he introduced himself by the buggy. "Most people call me Tally."

"Talitha." He almost whispered the name, weighting it with emotion.

"'Talitha' means 'little girl' in Aramaic. I suppose that's why I prefer Tally."

"I get it. I don't know what 'Franklin' means, but it makes me think of a three-piece-suit, corporate type who works eighty hours a week so he can buy stuff he doesn't need. I guess that's why I prefer Tripp."

"But Tripp isn't short for Franklin."

"I was Frankie for a time," he said. "I didn't mind it, but my grandmother had a different idea for my nickname."

Tally folded her hands in her lap and waited for him to continue his story. This was the first time in her life she'd been in the diner with an Englischer. That is, if she didn't count the Collinses. She had a vague sense she was doing something wrong—her grandparents would definitely think she was—yet guilt didn't prick her conscience now, even though it had over far less serious transgressions. Like the time she'd thrown an apple at Caleb and hit Marcus Fisher's oldest brother in the back instead. Caleb tried to take the blame, but guilt pricked her conscience until she confessed to the misdeed. Why was her conscience, which had been so sensitive then, so completely oblivious now?

"Have you ever heard the phrase 'trip the light fantastic'?" Tripp asked.

Tally took a moment to think. If she had, it would have been while she was spending time with the Collins family. But the phrase didn't sound familiar, and even the words themselves sounded foreign to her. "I don't think so."

"It's an idiom that simply means to dance in an imaginative way." Tripp gave that same self-conscious shrug again. "I've always loved music and dancing and singing. My grandmother used to say that someday I'd trip the light fantastic and be the next Fred Astaire. She was wrong about that, but the nickname stuck."

"Fred Astaire?"

A flicker of pity crossed Tripp's face but disappeared so quickly, Tally would have missed it if she'd blinked.

"He was a famous dancer. Long before your time."

"Why was your grandmother wrong?" Tally asked. "Did you change your mind about the singing and the dancing?"

"Let's just say, the time came when football was more fun. Now, keep in mind, I was nimble on my feet after taking all those years of dance lessons. I was the star quarterback at my high school and had big dreams of playing for a pro football team after college." His tone suggested that his dream hadn't come true.

"What happened?"

"My senior year, we made it to the state playoffs. It was a tough game between two powerhouse teams, and we were in the third quarter with a tied score." He'd grown more animated as he talked, but suddenly he stopped. After a moment, his self-deprecating laugh broke the awkward pause. "This is a story I love to tell the guys, but I'll spare you the gory details. Long story short, I busted my knee. No more football. No more dancing."

"That must have been devastating."

"It was," Tripp agreed. "But it was what it was."

"What did you end up doing instead?" Tally wasn't sure why she felt comfortable asking this stranger so many questions. It wasn't like her to be so openly curious about someone she didn't know. Maybe it was because he'd handled Scamp with such gentleness when he tucked him in his jacket. Or maybe it was because she was lonely and feeling misunderstood. After the past few days of upset, it felt restful to put the focus on someone else and temporarily escape her mixed-up thoughts and feelings.

"I drifted for a while," Tripp said. "But just because I couldn't dance didn't mean the music had left me. I ended up playing keyboard and guitar for a couple of bands that didn't go anywhere." His hands rapped out a rhythm on the tabletop. "Eventually I decided it was time to grow up, so I went to college and graduated with a business degree. Not long after, I got a gig managing an up-and-coming pop band."

The waitress arrived with their orders. Rivulets of the melting ice cream streamed across the golden crust of the pandowdy. Dark syrup laced the whipped cream that was dissolving in the steaming hot chocolate. Tally wrapped her hands around her mug to warm her chilled fingers.

"Do you mind if I say grace?" Tripp asked.

Startled at the request, Tally smiled and lowered her eyes. The prayer was short and simple—a blessing for their food and a request for favor and wisdom in the days to come. From the tone of his voice, that part of the prayer sounded personal. She wondered why he needed wisdom but didn't intend to ask. Though Tripp Thayer didn't seem to mind her curiosity about his past, she drew the line at prying into his spiritual life.

After he'd finished praying, they both tasted the pandowdy and agreed the blackberries were delicious.

"Tell me about your band," Tally said. "Did they become famous?"

"They had a couple early hits, but then things fell apart." As they ate their dessert, Tripp shared a few anecdotes about moving to faraway California to seek his fortune and what it had been like to travel from one city to another with young men who had too much talent and too little sense.

When he shifted the conversation to her, she told him about living with her grandparents and her love of growing plants and flowers. She also explained how, less than a week ago, she'd run into traffic to save Scamp from being hit by a car.

"When I reached the sidewalk, I fell on a patch of ice, and people took photographs of me on their cell phones," she said. "It was so embarrassing."

Tripp swallowed a bite of his dessert and then rested his fork on his plate. "I have a confession to make. I saw a few of those photos. They were intriguing."

She raised her eyes to his and was startled by the depth of emotion in his gaze. A strange tingle raced along her spine. What was she doing here with this stranger? This Englischer? Was visiting with him a mistake?

As quickly as the questions came to her, though, they dissipated. Maybe it was because they were in a public place, or perhaps it was the sadness she sensed in him that put her at ease. Whatever the reason, Tally's jitters quickly gave way to a sense of peace. She found that she wanted to know more about this stranger who might be an answer to her prayer. "Are you still a band manager?"

"I mostly write songs these days. Sometimes I produce an album for a friend or work behind the scenes at concerts. A television special here and there. About as opposite as you can get from the world of three-piece corporate suits."

"Do you still live in California?"

"I keep an apartment outside New York City, but mostly I live wherever Rosemarie and the road take me." His eyes clouded. "Rosemarie is my RV. I named her for my grandmother—the same one who decided Tripp was a better nickname than Frankie. That woman sure did love to travel."

"You drove here in an RV?" Tally could only imagine how freeing it must be to travel like that. She'd rarely stepped foot outside Lancaster County, though that was about to change. At any other time, a train trip to Florida would have been a dream come true. Now it was a nightmare.

"I was staying at a campground near Phoenix," Tripp said, "escaping the cold by basking in the Arizona desert heat, when I saw your photo. Before I could change my mind, I hopped a plane to Philadelphia, rented a car at the airport, and here I am."

"That sounds incredible. Traveling from Phoenix to Philadelphia on a whim." Tally was truly impressed, but also unnerved. He had made a trip like that because of a photo? Because of *her* photo? Once again, an inexplicable peace settled upon her.

"It was more than a whim," Tripp said softly. His quiet words carried a weight that neither of them seemed to know how to acknowledge.

After taking another bite of his dessert, he put down his fork and gave her a congenial smile that lifted the mood. "Do you ever travel?"

"I've been to Baltimore a couple of times," Tally said. "We're supposed to go to Florida tomorrow." She shifted her gaze to Scamp, still hidden within the folds of Tripp's jacket. Did she dare ask this man to take her puppy? Could she trust someone who traveled around in an RV—someone she'd just met—to care for him? To love him?

"You don't seem too excited. Don't you want to go?"

"It's creating a . . . complication."

"Anything I can help with?"

This was her chance. She opened her mouth to ask the craziest favor one stranger could ask another, but the words wouldn't come. "I don't want to talk about it," she said instead. "I'm sorry."

"Sure. I understand." Tripp pulled a photograph from his pocket and then slid it across the table toward Tally. "I'm not sure I should show you this. But since you're leaving tomorrow . . ."

She gave him a curious look, then picked it up. The picture had been taken years ago, but Tally recognized the older woman in the photo as a younger version of Grossmammi. In the photo, she lovingly smiled at the baby she held in her arms while the young woman beside her beamed with pride.

"Why do you have a picture of my grandmother?" she asked. When he didn't answer, she tried a different question. "Who is the woman with her?"

"Her name is Lila." Tripp's voice cracked, and he cleared his throat. "We met at a folk music festival in Iowa. She was the lead vocalist in a band with a couple of guys who had no idea what a treasure they had in her. From the first time I heard her sing, I knew I could make her into a star."

Tally mentally pushed against the obvious explanation of why Tripp was here, why he was showing her this photograph. All her life she'd wanted answers. Now that they seemed to be within her grasp, she wasn't sure she could bear to hear them. When she spoke, her voice was hoarse. "That doesn't explain why she's with my grandmother."

"I want to tell you the story, Tally. But it might not be easy for you to hear."

The bell over the door clanged as someone walked into the diner. When Tally glanced toward the sound, her gaze immediately met Caleb's. He started toward her with a warm smile, then shifted his eyes to the stranger. The smile faded into a concerned frown, and he hurried toward the booth.

"I saw Sprout outside," he said to Tally, then he stared at Tripp. "What are you doing here?"

Tally took care not to disturb Scamp too much as she scooted him over to make room for Caleb. "Please sit with us." As Caleb lowered himself to the bench, Tally introduced the men to each other.

"I saw you outside the hardware store yesterday. When Tally was inside the bank." Caleb's tone sounded accusing.

"I saw you too." Tripp's voice remained steady. He looked amused as he took in the sight of Tally and Caleb sitting beside each other.

"You didn't answer my question," Caleb said. "Why are you here? With Tally?"

"To give her this." Tripp pointed to the photograph of the two women and the baby.

Tally tapped the image of the older woman. "This is Grossmammi."

Caleb studied the picture. "I don't understand. Why would you have a photograph of Iris Byler?"

"I think I know." Tally closed her eyes and willed her anxiety to lessen. With Caleb beside her, she could face whatever Tripp Thayer had to tell her. She opened her eyes and pointed first to the younger woman and then to the baby. "Her name is Lila," she told Caleb, and then she shot a quick glance at Tripp. "And the baby she's holding is me."

CHAPTER SEVENTEEN

Caleb stared at the photograph, trying to wrap his mind around what was happening. He'd walked into the diner to search for Tally so he could pour out his heart. Finding her seated across the table from the stranger who'd been watching them yesterday had unnerved him. But if Tally was right—if she was the baby in the photo—did that mean the young woman in the photo was her mother? That this Tripp Thayer was her father?

"I took this picture on your six-month birthday." Tripp's voice was hoarse with sadness. "Lila hadn't known either of her grandmothers, and she wanted a three-generation photograph with her mother and her daughter. She carried a framed five by seven of this photo wherever she went and a smaller print in her wallet. I had this copy made for you, Tally. If you'd like to have it."

"I would. Danki." Tally couldn't seem to take her fingers from the photo. She held the picture as if it were a precious talisman that would disappear if she let it go. Caleb couldn't imagine what she must be feeling. He'd been born in the house he still lived in, and he'd grown up within a few miles of both sets of his grandparents. Dozens of his uncles, aunts, and cousins lived throughout Lancaster County.

Though Tally rarely mentioned her parents, he knew they were a mystery to her, their identities a secret known only to Aaron and Iris Byler, who weren't in any rush to share it. Now someone else—a long-haired stranger with the bearing of a man who could take care of himself in a fight—was finally revealing the truth about Tally's heritage.

More than anything, Caleb wanted her to know that he stood beside her. No matter what this Tripp Thayer had to say and no matter the repercussions when her grandparents found out about this meeting. He covered her hand, the one resting on the photo, with his, hoping she'd find strength in his love for her. She leaned her shoulder against his side. Never had they sat this close before, but Caleb wasn't about to shift away. She needed his closeness, and he would not put even an inch of space between them.

"Where is Lila now?" he asked and prayed Tally wouldn't be devastated by the answer.

"If it's okay, I'd like to tell you a little story first."

Tripp then told them about a talented singer with ambitions too big for her Iowa small town and the moderately successful band manager who planned to make her a star. While pursuing that dream, the two had fallen in love and married against the wishes of the singer's parents, who disowned their daughter until they learned she'd given birth to a baby girl. Finally, the grandparents reluctantly accepted the husband because they wanted to be part of their granddaughter's life.

But they still hadn't approved of his occupation or his ambitions for their daughter. From their perspective, anyone with a teaspoonful of sense knew the pursuit of fame was a devilish trap. They couldn't abide the thought of their granddaughter traveling with her parents from one town to another and another just so the talented singer could chase after a meaningless dream.

As Tripp talked, Caleb grew increasingly aware of the shifts in Tally's breathing and the tension of her body. When he cast a furtive glance in her direction, he saw that her cheeks were pale and her lips appeared dry. Her hand was cold despite still being covered by his warm one. Around them, the other customers and the waitstaff in the diner seemed to fade away, and even the clatter of plates and tableware seemed muffled.

"This next part is hard to talk about," Tripp said. "But I think you need to hear it."

Tally stiffened as if preparing to face dreadful news. When Caleb released her hand and placed his arm around her, she nestled into his shoulder. He nodded for Tripp to continue with the story.

"Lila was on the verge of signing a major contract to perform at a huge music festival in Nashville." For the first time, Tripp no longer pretended that the story wasn't about him and his young wife. "All our dreams were on the verge of coming true. We were on our way home after our big celebration when a deer ran in front of the car. I swerved, but the roads were slick from a storm that had passed by earlier, and the car slid toward the ditch."

He paused, running his hand along his face as if to wipe the memory away. His voice cracked as he stumbled over the words. "I couldn't get the car under control, and we rammed into a tree."

A muffled sob escaped from Tally's throat.

Across the table from them, Tripp hung his head and took a few deep breaths. When he looked up, he held Tally's gaze as Caleb tightened his grip on her shoulder.

"To make a long story short, I'd had a couple of glasses of wine with supper." Tripp shrugged, and the slightest smile flitted across his face. "After all, we were celebrating."

His mood immediately shifted from his sorry attempt to excuse himself to a more sober demeanor. "There was an investigation. I was charged with involuntary manslaughter, and the judge pretty much threw the book at me. Four long years. Lila's parents were given custody of my baby daughter, the only person I had left in this world."

He paused again and took a long drink of water before continuing. "They wrote to me the first few months. Even sent me pictures of my little girl. But then the letters stopped. A friend of mine drove to their house to see why they'd stopped writing, but they were gone. Just like that, they'd vanished into thin air." He snapped his fingers.

"The first thing I did after my release was to hire a private detective. But it was as if they'd ceased to exist. And then earlier this week I got a call from an old friend who happened to see a viral photograph of an Amish girl from Lancaster County who looked enough like Lila to be her twin sister." He paused to take a deep breath. "In my heart, I knew that girl had to be my Tally."

Tripp pressed his lips together.

"You're saying . . ." Caleb paused and cleared his throat. "You're Tally's father?"

Tripp held Caleb's gaze, then shifted to Tally. "Yes," he said, his voice a mere whisper. "It appears I am."

CHAPTER EIGHTEEN

Tally had braced herself for the words she expected Tripp to say. But hearing him speak them out loud sent a shudder through her spirit unlike anything she'd felt before. She was holding her arms to her stomach as if she were sick, and she felt as though she'd disintegrate into a pile of nothingness if she pulled a hand away to wipe back her tears.

A thousand thoughts raced through her head, but one truth stood out among the rest—her grandparents' greatest fear had come true. This unexpected encounter with her father had happened because people had used social media platforms to share her photograph on the internet. Though her grandparents didn't understand why the Englisch wasted time on such nonsense, they weren't totally ignorant of technology's reach.

Tally's photograph had been sent out into the world, a shameful occurrence in itself but one surely made more dreadful to Grossmammi when she considered whose eyes might see it. Her sudden eagerness to leave Lancaster County made perfect sense. Tally's grandparents had planned to run away from Birdsong Falls just as they'd run away from Tripp when Tally was a baby. Once again, they had plotted to take her away from the only parent she had left.

Caleb tightened his hold on her, and she closed her eyes as she rested her head in the crook of his shoulder. A sense of belonging swept over her, giving her strength even as she acknowledged and accepted her weakness.

"I don't understand. Why did they disappear like that?" Caleb asked the question that was stuck in Tally's throat. "If they had legal custody of Tally, you couldn't have taken her back from them, could you?"

"They considered me a bad influence. Maybe they were right. I certainly wasn't a teetotalling churchgoer. Not back then." Tripp shrugged, a gesture now familiar to Tally. "At least, that's how they saw me. And then I took their daughter from them. My guess is they didn't want history to repeat itself."

"All these years, they've told me nothing," Tally said. Her grandparents' silence had led her to believe her parents had either died in an unspeakable tragedy or abandoned her. Learning that her father had been alive this whole time, and that he'd searched for her, was like visiting the House of Mirrors at the Lancaster County annual fair. Tripp's revelation distorted both her sense of the past and her view of herself and her grandparents.

Tripp tugged one more photograph from his shirt pocket. "Here's another picture you might like to have. It's of your mother performing onstage at a music festival in Louisville. I took that picture about a month before the accident."

Caleb reached across the table for the photograph, and he and Tally looked at it together. Lila's oval face featured large brown eyes and delicate features, and it was framed by hair that fell all the way to her waist. She stood before a microphone, wearing a lime-green dress with a scoop neck, as she played a guitar and sang.

"You look so much like her," Caleb said, seemingly in awe at the resemblance.

"I do, don't I?" Tally's voice filled with emotion as she savored the image of the mother she'd never known.

"Lila had a gift," Tripp said. "Something about her voice, her music, touched people deep in their souls. Her parents . . ." He paused, as if choosing his words carefully. "They were good people. Hardworking, sensible people. Like I said, they believed Lila was chasing a dream that would only end in heartache."

Tally lifted her eyes from the photo. "But you didn't believe that."

"Fame is fickle." Tripp leaned forward and rested his arms on the table. "And there are no guarantees in the music world. What mattered to us was that we were taking that journey together. Rise or fall, we planned to grab whatever opportunities came our way."

He stared out the window, and then swiped his hand over his face. His eyes turned red. "They blamed me for her death. But no more than I blame myself."

Flames of anger flickered in Tally's heart. Her mother was dead, her father an ex-convict, and her grandparents were liars. All three of these facts hurt her, but in this moment, it was her grandparents' deception and secrecy that cut the deepest wound.

"They should have told me." The bitter words burst from her lips.

"I imagine they were trying to protect you," Tripp said quietly. "All they've ever wanted to do is protect those they love. Including Lila." Tally wasn't sure which of them he was trying to convince: himself or her.

"You're making excuses for them?" she demanded. "After all they put you through? Put *me* through?"

"I warned you this would be hard to hear." Tripp's voice sounded stronger now. "I imagine it's even harder to accept. Believe me, I had every intention of talking to your grandparents before I approached you. I wanted to ask their permission so they'd see I've changed. I've been hanging around, trying to work up the nerve to visit them. But when I found you crying in your buggy . . . I don't know how to explain it except that God prompted me to go to you. Just like I used to when you couldn't find your pacifier." He chuckled as a faraway look came into his eyes. "Your mom said I coddled you. But she loved me for it."

He returned his gaze to Tally. "It took me a long time to forgive Aaron and Iris for what they did. But I had a spiritual mentor in prison who helped me understand they acted out of fear. First they were afraid I'd take Lila into a world they didn't understand. And, truth be told, that's what I did. Then every parent's worst nightmare came true when she was killed. They love you, Tally, and because of that love, they couldn't take a chance of anything happening to you. They believed they needed to protect you from me, so they ran to a place I'd never think to look for you. An Amish settlement in the midst of the most populous Amish community in the country."

Tally hesitated, allowing his words to sink in. "It was still wrong of them," she insisted.

"I thought so, too, for the longest time. But now I believe their motives were more misguided than wrong. Love sometimes is."

Tally swiped again at her eyes. As Tripp had talked, the angry flames had quieted within her. She wasn't ready to absolve her grandparents of their guilt, but what Tripp said made sense. They'd failed to protect their daughter and were so determined to protect Tally that their judgment had been clouded. Though they rarely said so out loud, she knew deep in her heart that they loved her. She still loved them despite everything she'd just learned.

Forgiveness would come, but a part of her wanted to hold on to her righteous anger and hurt awhile longer. They owed her as much time as she needed to sort through this emotional mess. Didn't they?

Scamp squirmed within the jacket and yipped as he raised his head. Tally immediately lifted him onto her lap and shushed him. Taking him to Mr. Wray was no longer an option. It would be dark by the time she drove there and home again. Dusk was already settling upon the town.

Threads of stubbornness and resolve had knotted together within her. She'd bought Scamp, and he belonged to her. There was no longer any need for her grandparents to run off to Florida. They could still go if they wanted, but she intended to stay home. With her puppy and where she would be close to her friends.

Scamp wiggled free of the jacket and pawed at Tally's chest. "I think he's hungry. I hate to leave, but I should probably get him home."

"I'll take you," Caleb volunteered. "We can tie Sprout to the back of my buggy. Daniel and I will come back and get yours tomorrow."

Tally nodded her assent to Caleb, then stared at the man who sat across from her. Was the connection she felt with him real—born of forgotten moments that still lived within her heart—or was it a figment of her imagination, a manifestation of her longing for a father? "I can't face my grandparents on my own. Not now. Will you come with us?"

A range of emotions that Tally had trouble deciphering flickered in Tripp's eyes before his face settled into an expression of decisiveness.

"I have a rental car. If there's a place here in town to leave your horses, you could both ride with me."

"It's best if we take the horses," Caleb said. "It's slow-going, but perhaps that's Gött's way of preparing us for a difficult encounter."

"I understand," Tripp replied.

"Do you mind if I ask you a question before we go?" Caleb asked.

"You can ask anything you like."

"Were you ever Amish? Is your coming from outside the community the real reason the Bylers didn't accept you?"

"No. I never was Amish," Tripp said, "and neither were the Bylers. At least, they weren't back then."

Tally had sensed this might be the case when Tripp said her grandparents had hidden in a place where he'd never think to look. Still, hearing the words spoken aloud was like feeling the aftershock of an earthquake. The disclosure was not as startling as the initial revelation but still alarming. Was there nothing about her life that wasn't a lie?

Though at first she'd been glad of Caleb's offer to drive her home, now she didn't want to be alone with him. She wasn't ready to talk to him about what was going on inside her. How could she tell him what she was thinking when she hardly knew herself?

Scamp yipped again, and other diners turned toward them. "I can drive myself," Tally said to Caleb. "But I'd like you to be with me when I see my grandparents. If you don't mind."

"Of course." Caleb slid from the booth and reached for the puppy. "I'll follow you."

Tally turned to Tripp. "And you're coming too?"

Tripp didn't hesitate, not even for a second. "If you want me, I'll come."

Tally smiled at him for the first time since he'd started his tragic story, a small gesture to express her gratitude. This entire conversation hadn't been easy, and she couldn't imagine what her grandparents would think when she unexpectedly showed up with their son-in-law.

She drew a small amount of guilty satisfaction from the fact that she'd have the upper hand this time. The question of returning Scamp was nothing compared to the confrontation that was about to take place. Grossdaddi and Grossmammi would no longer be able to hide behind their deceit once Tally confronted them with the truth.

The thought of the impending encounter terrified her. But she took comfort in knowing she wouldn't be alone. Caleb had come looking for her and defied propriety by sitting close to her. She'd needed that warmth and comfort. Somehow she knew that whatever happened when Tripp and her grandparents met again, she'd need Caleb's strength—both in that moment and throughout all the years of her life.

And she hoped that Caleb would always be there to provide it.

CHAPTER NINETEEN

Tally drove her buggy into the barn, pulling far enough inside so that Caleb could follow in after her. Tally quickly unharnessed Sprout and led him to a stall. Caleb looped a feed bag behind Buttermilk's ears to keep her occupied while he was in the house. Tripp, who'd parked his car outside the barn door, joined them. Beneath his corduroy jacket, his shoulders slumped as if he carried the weight of the world.

"I'll come back later and brush you," Tally promised Sprout. She felt an urge to stay and give the horse a few strokes, but her hesitation to go inside the house was cowardly. Besides, her grandparents likely would have heard the car's engine. If she didn't go inside soon, Grossdaddi would come out to the barn. For reasons she couldn't articulate, Tally preferred her grandparents' reunion with their son-in-law to take place in the house.

"Are you ready?" Caleb approached the stall, clutching Scamp under one arm. Tally felt a smile rise to her lips. Over the years, she'd seen Caleb bottle-feed newborn goats while sitting on the barn floor and warm newly hatched chicks within his palms before placing them under a heat lamp. Now Scamp reclined along Caleb's arm, his chin resting on Caleb's chest, as if they belonged together. She wished she could take a picture of them. The comforting sight gave her one bright moment in her grim misery, and she never wanted to forget it.

"Tally?" Caleb placed his thumb gently against her cheek. "You don't have to go inside if you don't want to."

Tally gazed into his eyes and once again found them to be the wellspring of strength she needed. "As long as you're with me, I'll be fine. I'm just not sure what to say to them."

"They're the ones who need to explain," Caleb said. "Not you."

"Caleb's right." Tripp stepped toward them. "But I can go in first if you like. If there's going to be a scene, you don't need to witness it."

"Yes, I do," Tally said firmly. "I'm sick of secrets and lying. Mine and theirs." She raised her eyes to Caleb's. "I was supposed to return the money, not keep it. I'm sorry I kept that from you. Can you ever forgive me?"

Caleb tilted his head to one side as if deep in thought. "On one condition."

"Anything."

"You forgive me for not being there when you needed me."

Tally looked at him in surprise. "But you were. You went with me to Mr. Wray's farm so I didn't have to go alone. You're here with me now. I can always count on you. Always."

"But not when you needed a home for this little guy." Caleb bounced Scamp in his arms. "That's why I came to town looking for you. If you still need a home for him, I'll take him."

Tally reached out and scratched Scamp behind the ears, her eyes wide. "Your parents don't want another dog."

"They're not getting one." Caleb gave her a sly smile. "I've decided to move into the old Keller homestead. I want to make it my own until the time comes to share it with someone else." The meaningful look in his eyes caused Tally's cheeks to warm. The heat she felt only intensified when Tripp tried to hide his chuckle with an obviously fake cough.

"It'd be nice to have company," Caleb continued. "What do you say to the idea of me keeping him for you?"

"Yes," Tally breathed. "I say yes." Once again, Gött had answered one of her prayers in a most unexpected way. Scholars might not consider these answers actual miracles. But to Tally, that's exactly what they were.

Still carrying Scamp tucked under one arm, Caleb walked with Tally through the kitchen into the living room. Tripp followed behind them. As they entered, Caleb saw Aaron sitting in the recliner reading a copy of *Martyr's Mirror*. Iris was rocking and knitting nearby. They both looked up, their eyes wary-looking, as if they weren't sure what to say to their granddaughter or what she might say to them.

Iris focused on the puppy. "I thought you were taking him back to where he belonged."

"He belongs with me," Caleb said quickly before Tally could reply. "Tally said I could keep him."

"You're as foolish as she is." The chair rocked faster.

"I'm sure you're right," Caleb agreed while ensuring his tone remained respectful. After hearing Tripp's revelations, he'd had to adjust his own view of the Bylers. At the same time, he couldn't cast aside his lifetime of experiences with them. Despite what they'd done, they were still Tally's grandparents and valued elders in their Amish community. He could gain nothing by showing them less respect now than he'd ever shown them before.

Iris raised her eyes to heaven as if imploring God to pour sense into Caleb's head. As she lowered them again, she appeared to catch sight of Tripp, who stood behind him in the doorway. Her eyes grew round as she clutched at her chest. "What is he doing here?"

Aaron's mouth widened, and he struggled to put down the footrest and rise from his recliner. "This is my home," he said to Tripp, who'd stepped into the room. "You are not welcome here."

"I invited him," Tally said. "If you make him leave, I'll go too. Please don't force me into having to choose between you. I don't want to do that. Believe me, I don't."

"Choose between . . ." Iris stuttered. She tried to stand, then sank back onto her chair. "That man is a murderer."

"No," Tally said. Caleb could hear in her voice that she was on the verge of tears. "He is my father." She hurried to her grandmother's side and sank to the floor beside the rocker. Then she pulled the photo from her pocket and thrust it before her grandmother. "Look, Grossmammi. It's you and me and my Mamm. Your daughter. I know you loved her, but so did he. Please, I beg you. There can be no more secrets between us. None."

Iris's eyes glistened. As she lowered her face into her apron, her shoulders shook in silent grief. Caleb turned away, a part of him wishing he hadn't entered the room. He wondered if he should leave so that this pain-wracked family could navigate their way to peace in private.

"How did you find us?" Aaron demanded. "You never should have been able to find us."

"Because of me," Tally said. "Because of the photos online. He saw them."

Aaron stared at Tripp as if his nightmare had come true. Caleb felt at a loss—what could he say or do to alleviate the tension in the room?

Though he'd heard stories of shunning that had taken place in the past, the practice wasn't followed in their district. He couldn't imagine the pain of having his parents disown him because of his choices. Even though Tally's mother hadn't been raised in the

Amish ways, he believed she must have loved Tripp very much to go against her parents' wishes—to choose him over them.

In that moment, a revelation swept over him. As much as he loved and respected his parents, and as much as he depended on them for advice and wisdom, he knew that if they ever forced him to choose, he'd choose Tally. He deeply, truly loved her. With a certainty deeper than any he'd experienced before, he knew that she was meant for him, just as he was meant for her.

He shifted his gaze from Tripp and Aaron to where Tally knelt beside her weeping grandmother. Suddenly Iris gasped, and her body stiffened. With a jerky motion, she grabbed for the arm of her rocker, and then her body simply collapsed, falling from the chair to the floor. Tally's eyes widened in fear. "Grossmammi? Grossmammi!"

The next few moments passed in a blur. Everyone seemed to descend on Iris at once, but Tripp was the one who took charge. He ordered Tally to fetch a blanket and Aaron to get a glass of water. Iris's eyes were closed. Tripp dropped to the floor and placed his ear against her pale lips.

"Her breathing is shallow."

Tally returned with the blanket and a small pillow. Explaining that he wanted to loosen Iris's collar to help with her breathing, Tripp gently rolled the older woman on her side and unhooked the top clasp of her dress. Aaron returned with the water, the fear in his eyes matching that in Tally's.

Tripp tossed Caleb his cell phone. "Call 911. Tell them you need an ambulance." He checked Iris's breathing again, then raised her eyelids. "Tell them we'll meet them on the way. To be on the lookout for a white sedan."

Caleb did as Tripp instructed. As he repeated Tripp's instructions to the emergency dispatcher, Tripp wrapped the blanket around Iris's frail body. Tally bent down on the other side of her grandmother to help.

"I'm going to carry her to my car." Tripp met Tally's frightened gaze. "I only have room for her and one other person."

"Take Grossdaddi," Tally said. "I'll get his coat."

"Good girl." He glanced at Caleb as Tally left the room, his unspoken request as clear as if he'd said the words.

"We'll follow behind," Caleb assured Tripp. "I'll take care of her."

"Let's go, then."

Tripp lifted Iris as if she weighed no more than a Kinner. Still clutching Scamp, Caleb hurried before him to open the back door. Once Tripp had carried Iris over the threshold, Caleb set the dog in the corner of the mudroom. "Be good, little fella. I'll be back for you." Then he sprinted through the snow to help Tripp settle Iris along the length of the back seat. Tally hugged Aaron before he maneuvered himself into the front passenger seat.

As Tripp opened the driver's side door, Caleb held out his phone, but Tripp shook his head. "Hold on to it," he said. "I'll call you once we get to the hospital."

"We'll be there soon," Caleb replied.

Tripp glanced over at Tally, who stood on the other side of the car with her arms wrapped around herself, as if in protection against both the cold and her fear. He clapped Caleb on the shoulder and seemed about to say something. But then, apparently changing his mind, he turned away, slid into the car, and started the ignition. Caleb went to Tally and placed his arm around her shoulders as Tripp performed a slick three-point turn and headed down the drive.

"I put Scamp in the mudroom," Caleb said. "Can you tend to him while I ready Buttermilk?"

"I'll do that." She shifted away, opening a sliver of space between them. But even that sliver was apparently too much because she immediately turned back to him. Caleb opened his arms, enveloped her within them, and held her tight as the sound of her sobs poured into his heart.

☙

On the seat beside Caleb, Tally huddled beneath a double layer of quilts as he urged Buttermilk to maintain a consistent trot. The buggy was outfitted with an LED lighting system that increased their visibility, and one amber headlight enclosed in a pedestal lamp illuminated the road ahead.

As they neared the crossroads, another buggy approached from the left. "That's Daniel and Deborah." Caleb cued Buttermilk to halt and stepped on the brake pedal.

"Will you tell them what happened?" Tally almost managed to ask the question without her voice cracking. But the final syllables of *happened* were practically inaudible. Several years before, while she was spending an afternoon with Nicole, the two girls had watched videos of daredevils attempting to cross Niagara Falls on a tightrope. Today, Tally had felt like she was walking an emotional tightrope like that one. Throughout everything—the proposed trip to Florida, her worry over Scamp's fate, and even Tripp's appearance in her life—she had managed to stay on the rope. But after Grossmammi's collapse, Tally's balance had been shaken. She couldn't bear to think that something truly awful could happen to her grandmother. If not for Caleb, Tally would have been lost in an abyss of despair.

Daniel halted beside Caleb so the brothers were side by side, though facing opposite directions. Deborah sat beside Daniel, one hand resting protectively on her pregnant stomach. Eliza and Marcus Fisher leaned forward from the second-row seat.

"We're headed to the home place," Daniel said, referring to his parents' house. "Why don't you turn around and join us?"

"Iris Byler has been taken to the hospital," Caleb said. "We're going there."

"Oh, Tally, I'm so sorry," Eliza exclaimed. "What happened?" Eliza's concern added to the growing lump in Tally's throat. She didn't dare try to speak.

"She collapsed," Caleb answered for her. "You'll tell Daed and Mamm?"

"Ja," Daniel said. "We will pray for Iris."

"Danki." Caleb was about to leave when Tripp's cell phone rang.

"You have a phone?" Daniel's tone expressed surprise and alarm.

"It's not mine." Caleb pushed the necessary button to accept the call. "Hello?"

The murmur of Tripp's voice came through the speaker, but Tally couldn't make out his words. Caleb responded in monosyllables, then said, "I'll tell her . . . She's worried . . . We're on our way." He ended the call.

"What did he say?" she asked, her voice low.

"There's *gut* news. Your grandmother regained consciousness." Caleb gave Tally an encouraging smile. "Tripp said the ambulance met them soon after they left your farm. The EMTs transferred your grandmother to the ambulance, turned on the siren, and were gone. So fast that he and your grandfather never caught up."

Tally felt her heart relax for the first time in a long while. "How is Grossdaddi?"

"I'm sure he's fine. He and Tripp are in a waiting area for the intensive care patients. He said to meet them there."

"We should hurry," she said quietly, touching his elbow.

"Tripp?" Daniel asked. "Who's that?"

Caleb glanced at Tally before answering. She gave him an imperceptible shake of her head. Even if she was inclined to tell

Caleb's family about the sudden appearance of her father, this was neither the time nor the place to do so. That news could wait till after her footing was more secure on her swaying tightrope.

"We need to get to the hospital," Caleb said. After a quick round of goodbyes, they were back on their way.

Since it was Sunday evening, the town's streets were quiet. At this time of night, only Birdie's Café, a pizza place, a convenience store, and a gas station were open. The drive gave Tally much-needed time to get her emotions under control.

At a traffic light on the opposite side of town, Caleb turned right on Melody Lane. The hospital was located on the outskirts of town, and although Tally had passed by a few times before, she'd never stepped foot inside the two-story tan structure. Everything about the building, from the emergency entrance's huge sliding glass doors to the multiple rows of cheap plastic chairs in the reception area, intimidated her.

The receptionist, a middle-aged woman with a ready smile, guided Tally and Caleb through the process of having their photos taken for a visitor's pass. Once the passes were affixed to their clothing, she gave them directions to the intensive care waiting area.

"I'm glad you're with me," Tally said as they entered an elevator to go to the second floor. "The directions were confusing."

As the door closed, Caleb reached for her hand. "I'll always be with you, Tally. Whenever you need me."

His caring tone stirred Tally's heart. When she glanced at him, he returned her gaze with a warm smile that caused her to go weak in the knees. The day had been difficult for her—and she feared that it could get worse yet. But through it all, she'd been acutely aware of Caleb's strong presence.

When he'd walked into the diner, a chill gust of wind had entered with him. But Tally had felt only his warmth. She hadn't realized how much she needed his calming presence until he came through that door and sat beside her.

When the elevator reached the second floor, Caleb released Tally's hand. Neither of them spoke as they navigated the long corridors to the intensive care unit. After their names were verified, an attendant opened the heavy metal doors for them. Tripp was leaning against an open doorframe near the unit's entrance, but he straightened as they drew near. His uncertain smile matched Tally's own inner turmoil. She didn't know what to say to this stranger whose appearance had caused Grossmammi's collapse.

Though perhaps that wasn't fair. In the past few weeks, Tally had noticed subtle signs that her grandmother might be under the weather. But Grossmammi always had an excuse—she'd been exerting herself or she was tired or the cold weather caused her joints to ache. As always, she'd resented any attempts Tally made to ask about her health.

Caleb greeted Tripp with a handshake. "Is there any news?" he asked.

"They're running a few tests." Tripp lowered his voice. "I'm worried about Aaron. He hasn't been able to see her yet. The waiting is wearing on him."

"Where is he?" Tally asked.

"In here." Tripp gestured toward the room behind him. "It's just us in this one. Smaller rooms make it more private for the families." He flushed as he spoke that last word, as if it reminded him of the frailty of his connection with the Bylers. "Go on in, Tally. He needs you."

She walked in without any hesitation. When Grossdaddi saw her, he rose from his chair, and she fell into his open arms.

"Please forgive me," he murmured. "I'm so sorry."

None of the responses that flitted through Tally's mind seemed appropriate. She could tell him what happened in the past didn't matter, but that would be a lie. She could urge him not to think about anyone except Grossmammi, but how could any of them do that? Though Tally's grandmother was their primary concern, Tripp's presence was a reminder that her and Grossdaddi's long-buried secret had been revealed and that the fallout could only be temporarily ignored.

"We'll get through this together," she finally said, hoping he found comfort in that simple reassurance.

"Ja," Grossdaddi agreed. "Together."

Once their embrace ended, Tally held on to her grandfather's arm and sat in the chair next to him. Caleb walked over and sat on her other side. Tripp once again took up his position in the doorframe. All they could do now was wait for the test results.

And pray. They could pray.

CHAPTER TWENTY

A wall clock above an ornamental mantel marked the passing of time. The minute hand seemed to move so slowly, Caleb found himself checking its accuracy against his own pocket watch. Apparently, it suffered from the same doldrums. The minutes dragged by, and no doctor appeared to bring them an update.

About half an hour after Caleb and Tally arrived, Daniel appeared in the waiting room with his parents, Eliza, and Deacon Levi Fisher and his son Marcus. As they walked in, Aaron struggled to rise from his chair. Caleb stood and welcomed the newcomers while Tally tugged on her grandfather's arm, urging him to stay seated.

Tripp had walked into the room ahead of the newcomers. Now he stood by the mantel, his shoulders slouched and hands pushed deep into his pockets. Noting his family's awkward attempts not to stare at the strange Englischer, Caleb walked over to stand beside him.

"This is Tripp Thayer," he said. "He was, uh, visiting with the Bylers when Iris collapsed. He drove her and Aaron to meet the ambulance."

"A *gut* thing he did so." Aaron's voice shook as if the strain of talking was almost too much for him. "And he gave young Caleb his phone to call the ambulance. 'Every minute counts.' That's what that doctor said." He ran his hand along his beard as he softly repeated, "Every minute counts."

After Caleb had finished the introductions, Deacon Fisher said hello to Tripp. Then he sat near Aaron and talked to him in a low voice. To Caleb's relief, his parents engaged Tripp in a conversation about the weather and the condition of the roads. Eliza and Marcus moved their chairs closer to Tally.

Daniel drifted toward the door, and Caleb followed him. "Where is Deborah?" he asked.

"She stayed at the farm with Sadie," Daniel replied, "who is definitely not happy about being left behind." He narrowed his eyes and lowered his voice. "I saw that Englischer at the general store a couple of days ago. Who is he?"

Caleb glanced at Tally as he considered how to answer his brother's question. He was certain his parents and the Fishers wanted to know the answer too.

Tally's head was bent close to Eliza's while her hand rested protectively on Aaron's arm. Caleb wondered what the deacon thought of this. The Amish weren't a demonstrative people—especially in public—and particularly when compared to the Englisch. But Caleb certainly couldn't fault Tally for comforting her grandfather.

"Caleb?"

He turned back to Daniel. "He is someone the Bylers knew long ago. Before they moved here."

"I know you too well, *Bruder.*" Daniel's expression softened. "You speak the truth but not the entire truth."

"The entire truth isn't mine to tell."

Daniel scratched his neck below his beard. Like all Amish men, he'd stopped shaving his jawline the day after his wedding.

A year later, he still didn't seem comfortable with the growth. "Is he trouble?"

Another difficult question to answer. Perhaps it had been a mistake for Tripp to go to the Byler farm with Tally. If she had told her grandparents that her father was in town before he showed up at their door, Caleb considered, perhaps Iris wouldn't have collapsed. But how could any of them have foreseen her reaction? Since Tally didn't blame Tripp, Caleb couldn't either.

"I don't think so," Caleb said to his brother. "At least, he doesn't want to be. In fact, I'm glad he was there. He knew exactly what to do."

"Gött led him to you at the right time, then."

Caleb looked past Daniel toward the nurses' station, around which patient rooms had been built in a U shape. Unless she was somewhere getting tests done, Tally's grandmother was in one of those rooms.

Their community relied on home remedies or the midwife for most of their medical needs. But serious incidents like this one meant relying on the skill of the Englisch doctors and their machines. The cold sterility of the ward, the quiet footsteps of the nurses as they moved from one room to another, and the sheer size of the place all made Caleb feel small and insignificant. How did Iris feel, all alone instead of surrounded by her family and friends? Did she even know they were here, gathered together to support her, Aaron, and Tally?

"Mamm is already planning meals," Daniel said. "Is there anything Deborah and I can do to help?"

Caleb started to shake his head, but then a thought occurred to him. "We had to leave Scamp at the Bylers'. He's by himself in their mudroom."

"You mean that dog Tally rescued? I thought you said the owner wouldn't sell him for less than . . . you couldn't have spent that much money on a dog."

Caleb couldn't help but grin at Daniel's bewildered expression. "Not me," he assured his brother. "Tally. People who saw her photo sent her enough money to buy him. So she did."

"I'm surprised Aaron allowed that."

Caleb felt momentarily torn. He wanted to tell his brother the truth. And the circumstances surrounding Tally's purchase of Scamp weren't as personal as the fact that Tripp Thayer was her father. But both stories were hers to tell the way she wanted, when she wanted, and to whom she wanted.

"It's complicated," Caleb said. "Could you and Deborah take him for a day or two? Just until I can get settled at the old Keller homestead."

"What does that mean? Or is that complicated too?"

"Yes. And no." Caleb shrugged. "I haven't told Mamm and Daed yet."

"I won't say anything. And to answer your first question, yes. We'll take care of the puppy."

"Danki, Daniel."

When the brothers returned to the waiting room, the chairs had shifted. Tripp now sat near Tally, and Caleb's parents were seated close to Aaron. Caleb glanced at the wall clock and compared the time it showed to his pocket watch. Time still crawled as the vigil continued.

Everyone gathered in the waiting room fell silent when a tall, thin man carrying an electronic tablet walked in. He wore a rumpled dress shirt and a patterned tie beneath a white lab coat. He stopped near the door, his eyes roving over the group until they landed on Tally's grandfather.

"Mr. Byler?" His bearing projected quiet authority, and he spoke with an affable warmth.

"That's right." Grossdaddi gripped the armrests and stood. Tally longed to support him, but she knew any help from her would only embarrass him.

"I'm Dr. Bennett. Your wife is asking for you. I can take you to her if you'd like."

"Is she well?" The hopeful tone in Grossdaddi's voice echoed Tally's own guarded optimism.

"She's resting." His gaze took in the others, then landed again on Grossdaddi. "I prefer to speak to you alone about the details. Privacy regulations require it. I'm sure you understand."

"But these are our neighbors. Our friends." Grossdaddi gestured toward Tally. "She is my granddaughter." He glanced in bewilderment from Caleb's Daed to Deacon Fisher, then finally to Tripp. The tension around his eyes relaxed as if he'd found the solution to his dilemma.

Tripp stepped forward and extended a hand to the doctor. "I'm Tripp Thayer, here on behalf of the family. We're all very anxious about Mrs. Byler. If there's anything you can tell us that would alleviate our concerns . . ."

Dr. Bennett gazed around the group again before seeming to come to a decision. "It's probable that she had a heart attack. We'll run more tests in the morning. That's all I can say."

"Thank you, Doctor," Tripp replied. "That is helpful to know. Is it possible for Mr. Byler's granddaughter to accompany him to his wife's room?"

"Of course. Please follow me."

A whirlwind of activity suddenly kicked in. Caleb's parents promised to stop by the farm to check on the livestock, and Deacon Fisher offered to return the next day. Grossdaddi thanked them, then shuffled toward the door where the doctor stood. Tally started to follow but then hesitated when she realized Tripp wasn't coming too.

"I'll stay right here," he promised. "As long as you want me to."

She nodded and then stopped beside Caleb. "It's been a long day," she said too quietly for anyone else to hear. "You should go home."

He lowered his voice too. "Daniel promised to take Scamp for a few days. I'd rather stay here a little longer if you'll let me."

"Danki, Caleb. I'd be glad of that." Though she still felt worried about Grossmammi, Tally's heart felt lighter than it had just moments before. The hospital wasn't a foreign place to Tripp. He'd be nearby to talk to Dr. Bennett on their behalf. Caleb's presence also gave her peace. She hurried along the corridor till she caught up with Grossdaddi and then steeled herself with a quick prayer before entering Grossmammi's room.

The room was dominated by a bed with metal guardrails that stood at its center, covered in white linens. Against the far wall, a long bench with a cushioned back nestled beneath drapes drawn across a pair of windows. A chair, a nightstand, and a tray table were the only other items in the room. But Tally scarcely noticed any of these. Her attention was on the slight figure tucked into the bed. Grossmammi's graying hair, which she always kept gathered into a tight bun, was loose around her face. Tally couldn't help wondering what had become of her Kapp.

A tube snaked from Grossmammi's bandaged arm to a plastic bag hanging on a stand. Other machines monitored her vital signs, reminding Tally of the medical dramas she'd seen with Nicole. None of these, however, had prepared her for the reality of seeing her grandmother as the patient.

She and Grossdaddi stood beside the bed, watching Grossmammi's chest rise and fall in peaceful sleep. Tally had no idea whether they could touch her or what was expected of them, and she was sure her grandfather didn't know either. Dr. Bennett talked about the test results and said he hoped the hospital stay would be a short one. "The bench under the window pulls out into a bed," he said. "One of you may stay with her if you'd like."

"I'll stay," Grossdaddi said.

Tally wasn't surprised he so quickly volunteered. As far as she knew, her grandparents had never spent a night apart in all their long years of marriage.

After Dr. Bennett was gone, Grossdaddi pulled Tally into a side hug. "We will get through this, Talitha," he said. "Your grandmother will come home, and we will welcome your father into our family. No more secrets."

Tally loosely clasped Grossmammi's hand. Her grandmother's fingers, strong and nimble from thousands of hours of kneading bread and sewing fine stitches, felt cold to the touch. In the quiet of the room, the rhythmic beeping of a monitor offered Tally a strange kind of comfort. Within that quiet, she repeated her grandfather's promise, making it a promise of her own.

"No more secrets."

CHAPTER TWENTY-ONE

As Tripp drove to the hospital the following Wednesday, Caleb marveled at how quickly they'd adapted to a new routine. The plan for the two men to stay at the Byler farm had come together quickly on Sunday night after everyone else had gone home.

Since it wouldn't be deemed proper for Tally to stay at the Byler farm by herself, Aaron was on the brink of having Tally stay with her grandmother and going home himself when she decided to call Nicole. Less than fifteen minutes later, Nicole and her mother arrived with a bouquet of flowers for Iris's room. Tally had spent every night at their home since, and Nicole dropped her off at the hospital each morning so she could spend the day with her grandparents.

Caleb had volunteered to stay at the farm to care for the live-stock, and Aaron had insisted that Tripp stop wasting money on a hotel when he could stay at the farm too. Now, every morning Caleb handled the chores while Tripp happily made them both a hearty breakfast. One day, it was an egg, cheese, and sausage casserole with fried potatoes. The next, eggs with hash browns, bacon, and waffles. Though Caleb would never have said so out loud, the Englischer could cook as well as—and maybe even better than—most of the Amish women in their community.

At least twice a day, they visited the hospital to check in on Tally and her grandfather. In between these visits, Tripp went with Caleb to the old Keller homestead where he proved himself more than capable with a hammer and a paintbrush. After supper and evening chores, they relaxed in front of the fireplace in the Bylers' living room. Last night, Caleb had popped popcorn as a special snack.

Tripp also was helping Aaron navigate the financial aspect of a hospital stay. Since members of Amish communities don't have health insurance, Tripp negotiated self-pay rates and assisted with all the paperwork. Though Aaron generally preferred to handle his financial matters in his own way, he'd expressed appreciation for Tripp's ability to decipher the forms, ask the right questions, and get the needed answers.

As far as Caleb knew, the Bylers hadn't yet talked to Tripp or Tally about their reasons for disappearing all those years ago. But Aaron now showed absolutely no indication that he harbored any lingering ill will toward his former son-in-law. Caleb hoped that Iris, whose health was improving every day, felt the same way. It was possible she owed her life to Tripp's quick actions.

After Tripp had parked his sedan in the visitors' lot, he and Caleb made their way to the second-floor waiting room. Caleb never knew who they'd find there; he only knew that it was rarely empty. Deacon Fisher and his wife had stopped in Monday morning to pray with Aaron. Daniel and Deborah had come on Monday afternoon to assure Tally that Scamp was getting along fine with their cat, Socks. Other neighbors and friends dropped by, too, all of them anxious to show their support for Iris and Aaron.

Today he was surprised to find only Nicole there, sitting in a corner and flipping through magazines. She brightened as he and Tripp entered and gestured for them to sit near her.

"You'll never believe it," she said enthusiastically before they'd even had time to remove their coats. "Mrs. Byler is up and about and going for a walk. Actually, she's in a wheelchair being pushed by Mr. Byler, but just ten minutes ago we were all together in this very room. Mr. Byler hovers around her like an anxious little bee. They're so cute together."

Caleb had a hard time imagining Aaron as a bee or the Bylers as *cute*. Leave it to Nicole to make those observations. "That is *gut* news about Iris," Caleb said. "Is Tally with them?"

"Oh yes. The nurse told them about an enclosed garden near the courtyard they could visit. I doubt they'll be gone long. You'll wait for them to come back, won't you?"

Caleb glanced at Tripp. "I'd like to stay a spell."

"I don't have anything more pressing on my schedule," Tripp replied. "Think I'll go down to the cafeteria and scare up a cup of coffee. Either of you want anything?"

Nicole held up a bright pink travel cup decorated with yellow and purple flowers. "I'm good."

Caleb also declined.

"See you in a few," Tripp said as he left.

"He seems like a nice man," Nicole said when he was gone. "Though I never would have taken him for Tally's father."

"She told you." A statement, not a question.

"That first night." Nicole's bubbly demeanor seemed to dim as she recalled the difficult conversation. "She tried so hard to hold herself together, but then the dam broke. Mom made cocoa, and Tally told us the whole story. At least, what she knows of it."

Caleb wasn't surprised to hear that Tally had confided in her friend, or that she'd fallen apart after leaving the hospital. He only wished he'd been there to console her. As if she'd followed his thoughts, Nicole playfully tapped his arm. "Sometimes a gal needs another gal. And a mom, even if she's not her own."

"Tally has always felt a close bond with your Mamm."

"I've been happy to share her. Especially with Tally." Nicole leaned back and gave him a long, appraising look. "She told me she gave you the email from Indiana University."

In the silence that followed, Caleb peered out the window. Through its frame, he saw bare branches reaching into a cloudless sky, the tree's gray limbs prominent against a pale blue background. This is what the university press offered him. For his words to be framed, to stand out, to be read by others, perhaps to be memorized and talked about. Images and thoughts stood juxtaposed in his mind, a poem forming in his heart as he considered what he wanted to do.

He'd carried the email, folded now into a tight square, with him since Tally first gave it to him. In quiet moments between chores and late at night before going to bed, he'd read it over and over again. The paper had worn thin along its creases with his handling of it. So had his ability to distinguish between the meanings of the email and Tally's newspaper photos.

Common sense said they were two totally separate events. The university's offer had absolutely nothing to do with Tally's sudden and unexpected fame. Yet the two were inextricably linked in his mind. Both had happened at nearly the same time. More than that, both had illuminated lessons about pride.

Tally had faced the question of pride after seeing that her photos showed her to be an attractive young woman, despite a lifetime of being taught to abhor vanity. Now Caleb was facing his own pride. He felt deeply pleased that someone from a university considered his poetry worthy of publication. At the same time, he harbored resentment over the invasion of his privacy that had led to the opportunity. Strangers had pried into his innermost thoughts and feelings while evaluating his manuscript, without Caleb having agreed to such a thing. Other strangers shared Tally's photos with the world.

The #AmishAngel sensation would continue until another shiny new object came along to take its place. That could happen any minute. Given the short attention span of most of the Englisch, it probably already had. He couldn't control the internet—nobody could. But he *could* determine who read his poetry. And he knew that he wasn't ready to include strangers in his audience.

He shifted his gaze to Nicole with a sympathetic smile. The bright hope in her eyes faded. "You're going to say no."

"For now."

"The offer might not come again," she said in her singsong voice. A well-intentioned warning delivered with Nicole's typical upbeat enthusiasm.

"I know." Caleb released a satisfied sigh. "It's enough to know it came once."

"I respect your decision. But you have a gift, Caleb. Don't hide it away from the world forever."

For a moment, he said nothing. Deep in his heart, he knew the decision was right. And it would remain so until the day when he could stand steady in an appropriate, humble pride. One in which he could acknowledge God's gifts without being tempted to slip into a satisfaction that centered on him. One glorified God; the other glorified self.

"Will you email the editor on my behalf? Say the right words?"

"Of course I will. And I'll try to leave the door open. Just in case."

"You are a *gut* friend, Nicole. To Tally and to me."

"A girl does what she can." Despite her flippant tone, she seemed pleased by his rare compliment. "Tell me, though, what did you think of Tally's Christmas gift? Were you surprised?"

Caleb's spontaneous smile stretched his cheeks. He'd shown the book to no one, wanting to savor each individual poem for himself. The words took him back to places and events and feelings that he could relive over and over again. Perhaps that was the true reason he wanted to keep them to himself. Even the poems he'd given to others held special meaning for him.

"It is a gift I will always treasure. Danki for all you did to make it happen."

"It was all Tally's idea." Nicole practically beamed. "I only helped."

☌

When Tally and her grandparents had first entered the enclosed garden, she was reminded of the conservatories she had read about in historical romances. Large plants, including a waving palm and a towering ficus, grew in huge pots, and flowers had been planted in raised beds. The large space was bordered by the hospital's exterior wall on one side and glass walls on the other three sides, which curved upward to form a glass roof. Double doors opened to a courtyard enclosed by the hospital's four wings.

Grossdaddi wheeled Grossmammi's chair to a wrought iron table with a mosaic tile top. He and Tally took seats on either side of her. The results of her coronary angiogram, taken when she was admitted, had indicated blockage in the blood vessels leading to her heart. Dr. Bennett had concluded she'd had a mild heart attack and explained that she needed a procedure called angioplasty to open the affected arteries.

The medical terminology sounded like a foreign language to Tally. But after Dr. Bennett left them, Tripp had gotten on his phone and looked up websites that helped explain the tests and procedure. The surgery had taken place on Tuesday morning. Though it had lasted only about an hour, the wait had been interminable. By that afternoon, however, the color had returned to Grossmammi's face, and the snap was back in her eyes.

Now, only a day later, her health had rallied even more. In preparation for their visit to the garden, Tally had brushed Grossmammi's long gray hair, pinned it into a secure bun, and covered it with a new Kapp she'd bought the day before. If Grossmammi continued to improve, they'd be taking her home tomorrow or Friday. Tally couldn't wait for them all to be home again and back to their usual routine. Though taking Grossmammi away from the hospital also frightened her. What if she collapsed again?

Tally shuddered as the image of Grossmammi collapsing to the floor beside her rocker washed over her. The vision still came to her, unbidden, especially at night. If Tripp hadn't been there, precious moments would have been lost while she, Caleb, and Grossdaddi stumbled around trying to figure out how to help her. Looking back now, she realized that Tripp had sent Grossdaddi for a glass of water simply to give him something to do.

"Are you warm enough, Iris?" Without waiting for an answer, Grossdaddi adjusted the blanket Grossmammi wore around her shoulders.

"There's no need to fuss so." She frowned at him, but the appreciation in her eyes told a different story. "It's nice to get out of that room for a reason besides getting poked and prodded."

"It *is* nice to see you out of that room," Grossdaddi said.

Tally inwardly smiled at this rare glimpse of the affection her grandparents felt for each other. It was hard to believe that they'd once been her age, or that their hearts had once beat with the same hopes, dreams, and jitters about the future that now beat in hers. She had no family photographs of them in their youth. The only family photo Tally had even seen was the single three-generational photo that had been so important to Lila.

Tally had stared at it so often in the past few days that she'd memorized every feature of both her mother's and her grandmother's faces. The curves of their cheeks, the lines of their necks, the shape of their brows. Grossmammi had been in her midforties then, with the faint etchings around her eyes and her mouth that had later deepened into soft wrinkles.

Grossdaddi interrupted Tally's thoughts by clearing his throat. "We have much to talk about."

His simple words caused Tally's stomach to knot. He was right. Yet the events of the past no longer seemed as important as they had on Sunday when she brought Tripp home.

"But not now," she said. "We can wait until Grossmammi is feeling better."

"I feel fine," Grossmammi protested. She clenched her fist and pressed it against her chest. "It's the burden of the past that was killing me. I pray you can forgive us, Tally. We meant to protect you, but what we did was wrong." A tear coursed down Grossmammi's cheek. "The pain of losing Lila . . . I couldn't bear it. You were all we had left of her."

If this conversation had taken place on Sunday, when her anger and grief were raw, Tally might have retorted that she'd been all her father had left too. But fear that her grandmother might die had blunted that anger. Conversations with Tripp had softened her grief. He'd forgiven the Bylers, realizing he'd never have the peace that surpasses all understanding if he did not. His actions had proven that forgiveness to be genuine.

"They did what they did out of love," he'd said to Tally more than once as he encouraged her to forgive them too.

"I forgive you," Tally said, reaching for her grandmother's hand. Grossmammi's skin was cold, but her fingers had regained their strength. "I hope you'll forgive me too. For deceiving you about the money and bringing Scamp home again."

To her surprise, Grossdaddi broke out in a hearty laugh. "That pup sure does deserve his name. I hear he's a mischievous fellow."

Tally looked at him in surprise. "Caleb told me that he's getting along fine."

Grossdaddi dismissed her protest with a wave of his hand. "That young man cares too much about you to give you anything more to worry about. Though I also hear that Deborah is growing quite attached to him. You might think about getting him back as soon as we're all home again."

"Do you mean it? I can keep him?"

Grossdaddi nodded, and Tally switched her hopeful gaze to Grossmammi.

"As long as he stays out of my vegetable garden and doesn't chase the chickens."

"I'll do my best," Tally promised. She understood that their change of heart about Scamp was likely an effort to make up for the pain they'd caused by keeping her from her father. But she also believed what Tripp had told her: they loved her. And she loved them too.

"Now that that's settled, we should talk about the church," Grossdaddi said.

The church? Tally couldn't imagine what he was referring to. A heartbeat later, it hit her. "Because we aren't really Amish."

"I haven't talked to Deacon Fisher yet. I don't know what he or the bishop will think when they learn we've been here under false pretenses all these years. But your grandmother and I have already come to a decision."

Tally's heart tightened. Did they plan to run away again? Where would they go? Florida?

"We are accustomed to our life here," Grossdaddi continued. "The plain way is a *gut* way to live. Even if we are no longer welcome in the church, we will stay in our home. I will farm our land and build cabinets. I might shave off this beard to get a look at my chin again and put a phone in the house in case we have another emergency. But other than a few minor changes, our lives will stay the same."

"And if the church accepts us, there will be no shaving or phone in the house," Grossmammi said firmly. "I pray that they do."

"So do I, Iris, so do I." Grossdaddi turned his attention to Tally. "You have a choice to make too. We hid you away in this life, but that doesn't mean you belong here. You've not been baptized and joined the church yet. If you want to leave us, we will understand."

"Of course I don't want to leave you." Tally turned to her grandmother. "How could I? You need me."

"This isn't a decision to be made today," Grossmammi said. "Or too lightly. You are drawn to Englisch ways. As much as it pains me to say it, you may find that an Englisch life suits you."

"I didn't even leave home during Rumspringa. Why would I do so now?"

"Because now you know the truth," Grossdaddi said. "And I'm sure your father would like to spend time with you."

Tally already knew that was true. Tripp had talked about driving his RV to Birdsong Falls in the spring and parking at a local campground for a few weeks. She had encouraged the plan. But moving away from the only home she'd ever known was unimaginable to her.

Or was it?

The truth was, Nicole had options in her life that Tally had never considered claiming as her own. After graduating from the community college, Nicole planned to get a bachelor's degree in graphic design and marketing so she could open her own business someday. Marriage and a family were part of Nicole's dream for her future, too, but in a nebulous, *someday* kind of way. She had multiple options. As part of the Amish community, how many did Tally have?

Now, though, a door was opening for her. True, the Rumspringa door had been an option for the past few years. She hadn't been interested in opening it even a crack, though. She'd been certain that the only life she'd known was the only life she wanted.

But what if that wasn't true? How would she know if she didn't at least explore other possibilities?

She pushed those thoughts aside as they walked back to the intensive care unit. Tripp met them at the elevator, a coffee cup in his hand. His broad smile enveloped all of them in his greeting. "Caleb is in the waiting room with Nicole," he said. "I'd like to treat all of you and your friends to lunch if you'll let me."

"That's very kind," Tally said. Out of habit, she glanced toward her grandfather, who nodded his assent. "Danki."

Tripp bent down so he was at eye level with Iris. "You can come, too, if we can devise a plan to smuggle you out of here."

Tally hid a smile as her grandmother actually blushed at Tripp's teasing manner.

"I'll take a rain check," Grossmammi said in her usual bossy tone. "And I'll expect you to honor it."

"Yes, ma'am." Tripp straightened, a pleased smile on his face, and then winked at Tally.

The warmth flowing through her filled her heart almost to the brim. Tally knew that she'd always miss not having a mom of her own. But the family she'd always longed for was right here.

Gött had brought them together, and He had healed the deep wounds of loss and regret.

CHAPTER TWENTY-TWO

While Caleb went to the Byler barn to harness Buttermilk to the buggy, Tally walked Tripp to his sedan. Scamp trailed behind them, his gray coat damp under the lightly falling snow. Occasionally, the pup got distracted by a scent only he could smell. Mostly, though, he stayed close to Tally, who had saved his life—and changed her own—only a couple of weeks before.

Grossmammi had been released from the hospital late the previous week. Tonight, despite Dr. Bennett's orders for her to take it easy, she'd insisted on bossing Tally and Tripp around as they cooked his farewell dinner. When the family had sat together eating it, though, she'd admitted that Tripp's roasted chicken was delicious and even asked him to tell her his secret.

Christmas was a mere three days away, and Tally had hoped that Tripp would stay and celebrate the holiday with them. But he had a prior commitment in Los Angeles—something to do with a holiday special for a major television network. He'd stayed as long as he could, but he needed to catch an evening flight for the West Coast.

He'd said his goodbyes to Grossmammi, Grossdaddi, and Caleb in the house. Now it was Tally's turn. She'd been dreading the moment. Though Tripp had promised to return, the little girl inside her was frightened that she'd never see him again.

She felt thankful for the long hours they'd spent together over the past few days. Tripp had eagerly accepted her grandparents' invitation for him to stay on at the farm after Grossmammi came home, and whatever tension remained had eased with each passing day. Tally wasn't the only one sad to see him leave.

At the car, Tripp opened the passenger door and placed the canvas bag of goodies Grossmammi had packed for him on the front seat. From the clanking of the jars, Tally gathered that the bag contained an assortment of canned goods. Probably a loaf of homemade banana bread and a packet of oatmeal raisin cookies from the freezer too.

"Remember that the plane flies both ways." He closed the door and leaned against it. "You're welcome to visit me anytime."

"The Amish don't fly." Tally bit the inside of her lip as she held his gaze and willed him to understand what she'd left unsaid.

He slowly nodded. "You've made your decision, then?"

"I belong here." She shrugged, belatedly realizing she'd copied his habitual gesture. "I'm content here."

At that moment, Caleb led Buttermilk from the barn. He halted near the barn door to give Tally the private time she needed with her father.

"Does he know?" Tripp nodded his head in Caleb's direction.

"Not yet. I wanted to tell you first."

"I'm honored. Truly I am." His affectionate smile widened into a grin. "And for what it's worth, the two of you have my blessing."

Tally's cheeks flushed. "He hasn't asked me yet."

"He will." The knowing confidence in Tripp's voice renewed her blush. He chuckled and clasped Tally's hands in his. "Englisch dads usually hug their daughters goodbye. But I don't want to overstep any bounds here."

Tally bit her lip again, torn between a desire to be held by her father and a lifetime of refraining from physical affection. Lately, she'd gone against that teaching—with Caleb in the diner and with her grandfather in the intensive care waiting room. She raised her eyes and smiled at her father. "I've kept enough Englisch in me for that."

Immediately, she was engulfed in his arms. "We loved you so much, Tally. Always have, always will," he whispered.

A moment later, he let her go and walked around the car to the driver's side. He didn't look at her again until he'd fastened his seat belt and started the engine. Then he waved at her through the window, turned the car around, and was gone.

Snow fell gently around Caleb's buggy, giving the surrounding world a pristine gleam. In the long spaces between farms, all sound dropped to a soft whisper—from the swish of Buttermilk's tail to the low clop of her hooves on the snow-covered pavement. At any other time, the gleam and the whisper would have inspired a poem. But Caleb was too aware of Tally's presence beside him to pay attention to the images and phrases that now vied for his attention.

They hadn't said much since leaving the Byler farm. Tally had smiled at Caleb as she settled Scamp between them on the bench seat, but tears glistened in her eyes. He'd followed Tripp's tire tracks down the long drive, then steered Buttermilk in the other direction toward his home.

With Scamp now in Aaron's and Iris's good graces, Caleb no longer needed to move to the old Keller homestead. But since the idea had been planted, he wasn't ready to pull it up and toss it away. His decision rested heavily on what happened today.

As they passed the drive to the Schwartz farm, Tally looked at him in surprise. "I thought we were going to your house to make popcorn balls."

"We have another stop to make first."

"Is Eliza at the Fishers?" Tally asked. "Are we picking her up?"

"I don't know, and no." Caleb pressed his lips together and gave her a teasing smile. "I have something to show you."

"What is it?"

"Your Christmas present."

"Oh, Caleb." Tally's eyes glistened again. "You always know how to cheer me up."

"I don't know about that." Over the past couple of weeks, he'd failed to ease her heartache on too many occasions.

"You gave me strength when Tripp told me he was my father. And again when Grossmammi collapsed." She reached across Scamp to tuck her gloved hand into the crook of his elbow. "I'd have fallen apart that night if not for you."

The gesture and her tender words strengthened his hope that she'd made a decision about her future that included him. Soon he would know for certain.

When they reached the old Keller homestead, Tally laughed with delight. "I'd hoped we were coming here!"

Caleb flashed her a smile, then directed Buttermilk into the barn. Soon he and Tally were standing by the outbuilding door, Scamp in Tally's arms. "Stay here," he said. "And no peeking. I'll be right back."

He opened the door wide enough to slip through, then turned on the battery-operated lamps that illuminated the space. Once all the lights were on, he stood by the door to make one final inspection.

Tripp had helped him paint the shipboard walls a pale green with a complementary yellow border. The potting worktable Caleb had built stood in a corner between two windows. A grow-light system hung from the ceiling in the opposite corner, and shelves and cupboards lined one wall. A decorative sign took pride of place near the entrance.

The old proverb would be familiar to Tally. She'd understand, as he did, that the two of them had been laying their foundation for most of their lives—a foundation centered on shared memories and valued traditions, on trust and respect, and on the teachings of Gött. A foundation whose cracks had been smoothed over and made stronger through the gifts of forgiveness and grace.

Caleb slipped back through the door and found Tally jostling Scamp, who was eager to escape her arms. "Are you ready?" he asked.

"Ready."

"Close your eyes and give me your hand."

Tally feigned exasperation but did what he said. He took Scamp from her, then opened the door and carefully guided her inside. "Open your eyes."

Tally's eyes flew open, and her mouth formed a delightful O as she looked around the room.

"Caleb," she exclaimed. "It's beautiful!"

"Freulich Kristag, Tally."

"This is mine? Truly mine?"

"All yours."

She removed her gloves to run her bare fingers along the sanded shelves. Then she moved to the potting worktable and exclaimed over its craftsmanship and utility. "If I could design a bench, I would make it look just like this one." Then her eyes landed on the sign, which glowed gently under the golden light streaming in through the window behind her. She read the words aloud.

A happy home is more than a roof over your head.
It's a foundation under your feet.

Caleb placed Scamp on the floor and took Tally's hands in his.

"Will you make a happy home with me, Tally Byler? Here at the old Keller homestead?"

"I will, Caleb Schwartz. My life is here, not among the Englisch, but with you."

Caleb's heart raced as he gently wrapped his arms around her and lowered his lips to hers for a first kiss that both satisfied and demanded more.

At their feet, Scamp barked his approval.

Up to this point, we've been doing all the writing. Now it's *your* turn!

Tell us what you think about this book, the characters, the town, or anything else you'd like to share with us about this series. We can't wait to hear from *you*!

Log on to give us your feedback at:
https://www.surveymonkey.com/r/LancasterRomance

Annie's® FICTION